SHIRLEY NOLAN

I0617586

LOTUS

SHAMROCK PUBLISHING

Copyright © 2016 Shirley Nolan

All rights reserved.

ISBN: 978-0692450420 (Shamrock Publishing)

ISBN-13: 0692450424

Lotus

Shirley Nolan

DEDICATION

For my children:

Cindy, Catherine, Barbara, John, Carol, Shelby and Grace

ACKNOWLEDGMENTS

If not for my wonderful critique partners and friends this book would never have been written. Thanks to Kathleen Ruth and Connie Grudzinski for the love, guiding and pushing. You are my dear friends and confidants.

And a special thanks to my husband, Ron Amador, who put up with me and encouraged me along the way.

Shirley Nolan

ONE

AS I STEPPED OUT OF THE TAXI IN FRONT OF A LITTLE store in Chinatown, I was filled with emotion. I was happy to be in San Francisco after a long voyage from China but I was also apprehensive about how much my life was going to change. My young husband, Chi, and I have longed for the "American Dream" since I could remember. We had been married for six months now and Chi wanted a career in America. I wanted an education, but the main reason we left China was that we wanted more than one child, the rule in China. I had been sick on the ship, and feared I was already pregnant with our first child. I told Chi my suspicions of pregnancy, and he was overjoyed, and expressed a desire for me to be a wife and mother only. He was a traditional man, and I had a lot to overcome if I were to attain my dream of an education and a career of my own. Although I wanted children at some point, I felt this may be too soon. The date was October 17, 1988.

The little shops looked crowded, and chickens and ducks hung in the windows of the small grocery stores. How very strange! Most of the people passing by looked Chinese but there were people of all nationalities.

We gathered our luggage and boxes. We had brought a couple of boxes with us that contained basic bedding, towels, a few cooking pots and dishes. The cab driver helped Chi unload the one trunk we brought. Chi paid the driver, and we walked into the grocery store carrying what we could. Chi left the trunk on the sidewalk until he could put the boxes down and retrieve it.

A man walked up to us with a smile on his face. His eyes were soft, dark, and very friendly. "You must be the Wah's, we were expecting you," he said.

He helped Chi bring in the heavy trunk.

"I will show you to your apartment in just a moment. By the way, your parents paid the rent for six months, you will just have to pay the utilities," he said. "Let me introduce you to my wife, Mrs. Ling." He said this in Chinese.

A stern looking Chinese woman stood at the counter talking to a man. Her facial expression startled me. She did not look kind at all. She frowned at me, her mouth turned down, and she did not smile. She looked angry and I wanted to retreat from her stare. As I looked at them, the man turned towards me. He had the bluest eyes I had ever seen. I wasn't used to seeing blue-eyed people so I couldn't help but notice. He looked straight at me and I diverted my eyes. Chi was busy with the luggage and didn't seem to notice him at all. Mrs. Ling walked over to us, and looked us up and down like she was judging us. I took a step back and wanted to sink into the ground.

"I don't want any noise up there," she growled at us. "No loud parties or you will be out on the streets.

"We are very quiet people," I said rather meekly. "We don't even know anyone here to invite over."

Chi didn't say a word. He seemed to be as shocked as I was by her attitude. *Why was she so mean to us? She was judging us before she had a chance to know us.* I was tired and the nausea returned I had felt on the ship. All I wanted to do was go up to the apartment and get away from this woman.

"I'm Chan-lei," I said gently. "And my husband's name in Chi." Chi still remained as if he were tongue tied.

"You may call me Mrs. Ling," she seemed to spit venom with her words.

Mr. Ling took us upstairs. We walked into the apartment, and I was disappointed and suddenly homesick. The apartment was dingy and small; everything looked brown and drab, and it could use a good cleaning. It smelled musty, like it had been closed up for a long time. Mrs. Ling came up behind us.

"Once again, I must tell you to keep this place clean and be quiet," she chastised us. "I have worked hard cleaning, and I don't want you to mess it up."

It was not clean, and I would be the one to work hard the next few days to make it that way.

"We will be clean," I said with my teeth clenched.

Chi finally spoke up, "You will find us to be clean, quiet people." With that, she turned on her heel and went down the stairs. Mr. Ling handed us keys and with a sad smile; he also went downstairs, finally leaving us alone.

My eyes filled with tears as I said to Chi, "This place is dirty and ugly."

Chi put his arms around me. "I know," he said "The furniture is old and worn but it can be made to look cheerful with a little work."

"I'm not sure there is any hope for this place."

"You will make it clean and cheerful, Chan-lei," he said abruptly. "I don't understand Mrs. Ling's attitude, but she must be a very unhappy woman. Mr. Ling seems nice, although somewhat embarrassed by his wife.

Finally, I smiled. We looked around the apartment. There was a small kitchen, bedroom, and bath, but the main living room was surprisingly good sized. The furniture was worn and looked like it had seen better days. The floors were wood and dull. I looked through our trunk and found linens for the bed, made up the bed, and it looked a little better, but not much. I thought of my parent's clean and colorful home. I would make cushions and buy colorful rugs for the floors, but first I would clean everything I possibly could in this ugly place.

"I'll go down to the store and buy some food for us," Chi said. You haven't had anything to eat all day. I think it is important for you to keep your energy up. Also, I will buy some cleaning supplies."

"Thank you, Chi, I need a hot bath, and there is no way I will get into that dirty bathtub,' I said, as I watched him go out the door.

After Chi had left, I sat down on the floor and began to cry. I didn't know why I was crying. *I'm here in America, where I had dreamed of being for so long. I can make this work,* I thought as I wiped away my tears and put on a pleasant, brave face.

Chi came back with groceries for dinner and cleaning supplies. He looked through a couple of boxes and found a wok. He was a genius with food and soon had a delicious stir-fry dinner ready. We ate at the small, plain kitchen table, but tomorrow I would find a cheerful tablecloth, and it would look so much better. After eating I felt much better.

After dinner, I cleaned up the kitchen and longed for a hot bath while Chi rested.

After cleaning the bathtub, I relaxed in the bath and thought of all I wanted to do the next day. First of all, clean the rest of the apartment and then Chi and I would go shopping. I thought about how much nicer the apartment would look with colorful cushions and at least one new rug. I brought some fabric with me from China, but mostly for clothing.

I woke up and looked around the strange room. Chi was not in bed, beside me, but I heard a noise from the kitchen. The bedroom still looked dowdy, but today I would fix that. Getting out of bed I looked out the small window. It was foggy and looked cold outside. I dressed quickly and went into the kitchen where Chi was cooking breakfast for me.

"Good Morning Chan-lei," Chi said smiling. "How did you sleep?"

"I slept well, all night. I feel so much better," I answered. "I'm eager to get started on our first real day in America."

"I'm going to go to the restaurant and introduce myself this morning," Chi said. "You should rest until I get back and then we can do some shopping."

That would work for me. I could do some more unpacking while Chi was gone.

"Chi," I said, "I know that speaking Chinese is easier for us, but I think we should speak English to each other most of the time. That way we will learn to be comfortable with the language."

"That is a wonderful idea. Why are you always so smart?" Chi said this in English and I laughed.

Chi left, and I was alone in the apartment. I scrubbed the kitchen and started to unpack some of the boxes we brought with us. My parents would be shipping more of our belongings soon. I missed them so much. The plan was for them to join us here and I could hardly wait.

It didn't take long to put our few belongings away. Now, our little home seemed to shine except for the floors. I needed to find a something that would perk them up. Chi was taking a long time, so I decided to go down to the store and buy some snacks and look for a cleaner for the floor. That would leave us more time for other shopping this afternoon. I changed my clothes, putting on a very pretty Chinese dress.

Entering the store, I felt the cold eyes of Mrs. Ling on me. Why doesn't she like me? I retrieved a basket and began putting groceries in it. Mrs. Ling made me feel very uncomfortable, but Mr. Ling gave me a warm and inviting smile.

The door opened, and a beautiful girl entered. She was Chinese, but looked Americanized. Her short hair was cut in a sort of choppy style with little pieces sticking up. I had never seen a Chinese girl with hair like this. My hair was long, straight and hung almost to my waist. She was wearing jeans and a silk shirt, not the usual Chinese attire. She seemed to float through the store like a little pixie. I had never seen such an adorable girl. She smiled at everyone and looked so happy.

As I passed her in an aisle, she looked at me and said "Hi."

"Hi," I said back to her.

"My name is Jenny," she smiled.

"My name is Chan-lei," I said a little nervously. "I just arrived from China yesterday. I studied English in school, but I'm afraid it is not very good."

"You speak English very well," she reassured me. "I was born here; my parents emigrated from China long before I was born."

"My husband and I have a lot to learn," I laughed.

"You're married?" she asked with surprise in her voice. "You're young to be married. I'm a student at San Francisco State University, a Political Science major, and planning to go on to Law School. I still live at home with my parents, not planning on marriage for a long, long time."

"Chi and I have known each other most of our lives. I'm twenty years old. We have been married for about six months now."

"You look even younger, she said. "I just turned twenty myself."

I instantly liked this girl, she had such confidence and seemed to be all I want to be. I wanted to go to college and study as she was. But I thought this might have to wait since I was probably expecting a baby and Chi was not thrilled with the thought of me going to school at all.

I didn't say anything about the baby. I wanted to get to know her better before telling her all my secrets.

"Do you have family here? Jenny asked.

"Just a distant relative that I have never met," I said. "But both our parents plan to join us as soon as possible."

"I can help you get acquainted and teach you things you don't understand," Jenny said gaily.

We talked a little longer and then Jenny gave me her phone number. I told her I would call her as soon as we had a phone. She said I was welcome to visit her house anytime. I couldn't quite believe how kind and friendly she was. I had only been here for a day and already felt I had a friend. Life in America was going to be good. Hopefully everyone would be as nice and friendly as Jenny.

I paid for the groceries and went back upstairs to the apartment and put the items away and before long Chi came in, grinning.

He was carrying a very large package. He sat it down and asked me to open it. I quickly opened the box and gasped.

"Chi, you bought us a television? Do we have money for such luxuries?" I said.

"I thought if we wanted to perfect our English, watching American TV would help us," he said, "and we do have a little money to spend."

I was so excited I could hardly speak. He put the television on a little table in the living room and put something he called "rabbit ears" on top. He turned it on, and it worked!

"Chan-lei," he said, "I told you to rest, but it looks like you have been working while I was gone."

"I went to the store and bought groceries and a product to clean this dirty floor. I met the most adorable girl, about my age. Her name is Jenny, and she was so kind to me," I chirped. "I think I already have one friend here."

"Be careful about making friends so fast," he said.

I didn't like being chastised by him, but I didn't say anything. I didn't want to spend all my time alone in this apartment while he was working and making friends himself.

"I saved the big news for last," he said. "The restaurant hired me. I start tomorrow as a Junior Chef. The pay is not wonderful, but it will do for now. I also stopped by the phone company and arranged for a phone for us. I don't want you alone in the apartment without a phone."

I fixed a little meal for both of us and then we went shopping. Chi was a master chef but he liked it when I cooked. We went to the shops in Chinatown and found most of what we needed. I was eager to venture outside of Chinatown, but Chi felt we were better off staying close by today. In one shop, I found a colorful rug for the living room. It wasn't expensive, but nice. They agreed to deliver it to the apartment for a small fee. Then we went to a fabric store where I found some fabric to make cushions for the sofa and chair that should hide how ugly they are.

As we were walking home, Chi said, "Why don't you ask Mrs. Ling to recommend a doctor?"

"Oh no," I said. "That woman doesn't like me; she would probably send me to the worst doctor in San Francisco. I will ask Jenny when I see her next. I didn't tell her about the baby yet. I get the feeling she thinks I'm too young to be married, let alone pregnant. I think girls marry much older here than they do in China."

"Remember, don't be so eager making friends, you have plenty of time," Chi cautioned me for the second time.

"I think she is very nice," is all I could manage to answer back.

I was appalled that Chi would not like me to make friends. It bothered me for the next few days, but I kept myself very busy making cushions and decorating the apartment. Since I didn't have a sewing machine, I had to do all my sewing by hand. I also ventured out into the neighborhood by myself to do a little shopping. There were so many different people on the streets. Everyone seemed so friendly and some were wearing traditional Chinese clothes like me, but I still felt that I stood out as a foreigner. The little shops were full of bright colored items. I found some bottles and dishes that added to the cheer of the place. Chi never complained when I spent money on our home. When I had finished, I thought we had a darling little place, so different than when we first walked into it.

Now I was ready to explore the city. The phone was installed, and the first call I made was to Jenny and we agreed to meet the next day at a café about a block away. My life in America was beginning. I had so much to talk to Jenny about, our trip to America, my wonderful parents, and my plans for the future.

Maybe I could talk to her about Chi's traditional ways and how much I wanted a career? Should I tell her about the baby that was probably on its way? It wasn't that I was sad about a baby, I wanted children eventually, but it seemed too soon and I wanted to do more with my life.

TWO

I WAS EAGER TO GET CHI OFF TO WORK THE NEXT MORNING. I didn't tell him I was meeting Jenny, but I did tell him I was going to do some shopping for American clothes. He understood when I said I felt out of place in my traditional Chinese clothes. As soon as he left I quickly cleaned up the kitchen and looked through my wardrobe to see what I had to wear. Why didn't I have a pair of faded jeans? I didn't have any pants to wear at all, much less faded jeans. I needed to do some shopping to fit in. I settled on my usual uniform, a simple black brocaded Chinese dress.

I was ready way too early, so I watched a little television passing the time. There was a news show on, and they were talking about crime and gangs in San Francisco. They said something about the Asian cartel in Chinatown. *Goodness, could be gangsters living right here?*

Finally, it was time to meet Jenny. I almost ran down the street to the little restaurant where we had agreed to meet. The streets were crowded with many people. When I entered the door, I saw Jenny sitting at a table. She jumped up and seemed to float through the air like a little sprite to meet me.

"I'm so glad to see you, Chan-lei, come and sit down." Her voice was as light as she was.

We sat down at a small table, and the waitress came over to take our orders. Jenny ordered a salad, so I followed her lead and ordered the same for myself.

"Now tell me all about yourself," Jenny said. "Why did you and your husband decide to come to America? What are your hopes and dreams, just everything?" she asked with a laugh in her voice. She seemed so eager to hear all about me and I equally wanted to know about her.

"Chi and I have dreamed of coming to America since we were children. And when we decided to get married it became more than a dream. Chi wants to be a chef in an upscale restaurant. And I want an education but most of all we didn't want to live in China where we could only have one child and be restricted as to how we could worship. We saved money and our parents helped us to be able to come here."

"I understand," Jenny said.

"I want an American education," I told her. "I love learning. I've thought about becoming a lawyer, but maybe that is just a dream. I might study something in the arts because my husband does not seem to agree with me. He is traditional and wants me to stay home and be a wife and clean house. I'm not sure why I'm telling you all this, but I want more than he does. He seems to concentrate on his own career. He thinks I should be content to be his wife."

Jenny reached over and patted my hand. "Maybe he will change his mind when he sees how women are here."

"I also need to buy some American clothes." I laughed looking down at my traditional dress.

Jenny laughed and said, "I can help you with the clothes, let's see you are so small, I would say you would wear about a size 0."

Although I had just met Jenny, I felt like I had known her for years. I smiled and decided to tell her my secret.

"I don't know about American sizes, but any size will probably not fit for long. Jenny, I'm pretty sure I'm pregnant. I was sick on the ship and now I still feel the nausea."

Jenny did not seem to show surprise like she had when she found out I was married. She just simply asked, "Have you seen a doctor yet?"

"No," I answered. "I was hoping you could help me with that too."

"I believe I can," she smiled. "It just so happens that my mother is an obstetrician."

"A what?"

"A baby doctor, she delivers babies."

Jenny went on tell me how sweet and lovely her mother was. "She is probably my best friend," she said smiling.

We had so much in common already. My mother was my best friend as well. I thought of how many girls told terrible stories about their mothers. I could never do that. My mother would do anything for me. I loved her so much and was missing her more than anyone could imagine.

"I can talk to my Mom," she said, "and make an appointment for you. She has an office downtown, but she also has a small office in our house. You can come there."

"Jenny, I'm scared. I wish my mother was here with me. I have always wanted children, but I think this is too soon."

"I think you will feel better after you see my mother. She believes all babies are a gift from God." Jenny said so sweetly.

Somehow I felt better already. Jenny was so sweet and kind.

We talked about where they lived in Pacific Heights, very different from Chinatown, Jenny explained.

"I will come over to your place and take you to my house so you won't get lost," she smiled.

We sat talking for a little while. I liked this girl. I thought of what Chi had said about making friends too soon and thought he was completely wrong. I would tell him about Jenny and her mother.

"Let's go look in some of the shops," Jenny said.

"Okay, but first I have to go to the bathroom."

Jenny pointed to where it was. As I got up, I caught my shoe on something on the floor and started to fall. Suddenly a strong arm caught me and stood me up. I looked into the face of the man I had seen with Mrs. Ling in the store. His eyes were like nothing I had ever seen; they were blue with flecks of green. A sudden flashback took me to when we arrived in San Francisco, his eyes were the color of the sea on the day we pulled into dock. They had a slight slant to them but were more almond shaped. The rest of his features including his dark auburn hair were near perfect. He had a faint Asian look to him, but also looked Caucasian. All of this I saw in a flash of a second. My heart did a little flip that I had never experienced before; he was the handsomest man I had ever seen. I thought he was gorgeous.

"Are you alright?" he said in perfect Chinese.

I could only manage to shake my head yes. *What was wrong with me? I couldn't speak.*

I hurried to the bathroom and ran cool water over my face. After I returned to the table, I was more in control of myself.

"Who was that? I asked Jenny. He doesn't look Chinese, but he speaks perfect Chinese"

"Eric O'Malley," Jenny said. "He was born here in Chinatown. His mother is Chinese, but his father was Irish. His father died a long time ago. Chan-lei, be careful of him, word is he is connected."

"*Connected*?". I had no idea what she was talking about.

"What does connected mean?" I asked.

"That he is part of the drug trade," she answered. "I have no proof that he is, but that is the gossip around town."

We left the restaurant and went to a couple of shops where I found a pair of jeans and a couple of shirts. I didn't know how long I could wear them, but I bought a size larger.

I hurried home with my purchases and hoped that Chi would like them. I cooked rice and meat for dinner. It had been a perfect day; Jenny, finding a doctor, and buying new clothes. Life was beginning for me here.

I was still in the kitchen when there was a knock at the door. Mr. Ling stood there with a large package in his arms.

"Come in," I said.

He brought the package in and put it on the floor.

"Goodness," he said, "the apartment looks beautiful. I can't believe how much you have improved it."

"Thank you," was all I could manage to say hoping he would tell his wife how lovely the place looked. So much for her saying to keep it clean, I laughed to myself.

The package was from my parents. Tears came to my eyes as I sat down on the floor to open it. It contained some of our household supplies, towels, sheets and some more of my clothes. Then I opened a little package all wrapped in pretty paper. It contained fabric, beautiful silk of different colors. A piece of red silk caught my eye. It would be perfect for the traditional Chinese dress, I thought, but it would also be nice for a blouse or shirt to go with my new jeans. My mother always knew what was right for me. I held the silk to my cheek and started to cry even more, I missed her so much. I hoped Jenny's mother would be as special as my mother, but didn't think that was possible. Oh, I could hardly wait until my parents joined us here. How could I go through having a baby without my mother here to help me? I was suddenly so homesick I felt ill.

I cried for a while and then washed my face before Chi came home. All of sudden, the blue-eyed stranger came to mind. *Why did I have such a reaction to this man? Even when I thought of him, my heart did flip-flops. What was wrong with me? I was a married woman and supposed to have thoughts like this for my husband, not some stranger. We were probably having a baby; we would be a family soon. And was the blue-eyed man really connected?*

Thoughts were racing through my mind.

It wasn't long befoe Chi came in with his arms restaurant and full of packages. He had brought food from the me a bouquet of lilies. They were beautiful.I put them in a glass of water, not having a vase. I made a mental mote to buy a vase. The flowers made the apartment look even more cheery.

"A package came from my parents today," I told Chi. "I think Mr. Ling was impressed with the apartment when he brought it up."

"Very good," Chi said, "and how was the shopping trip?"

"I bought some jeans like all the American girls wear and a couple more outfits. Don't worry, I didn't spend much money." I took a deep breath and said, "I also met Jenny for lunch. She is so nice, and I got to know her a little better and guess what? Her mother is a baby doctor, she delivers babies. I'm going to see her next week; Jenny is making an appointment for me."

"Oh Chan-lei, I don't care how much money you spend. I do worry about you being so trusting with people so soon, but pleased you are finally seeing a doctor. If you don't like her, we will find another."

"Jenny says her mother is nice. I have a feeling that Jenny is close to her mother that same way I am to mine. I think I will like her, I certainly hope so."

Chi gave me a hug, and I was happy, happy that maybe he did understand how much it meant to me to find a friend like Jenny. Happy that he understood how much I missed my mother.

Jenny called the next day and said her mother could see me the following Wednesday, she would come to my apartment about 10:00am.

I had several days to myself before my appointment. After seeing Chi off to work each morning it didn't take long for me to do my housework. I found a laundromat close by and washed the dirty clothes and sheets. I felt homesick and missed my mother so I had to keep busy with something so I wouldn't dwell on my loneliness.

I took out the beautiful silks my mother had sent me and held up the red piece. *I will make something out of this first*, I thought. I will have to sew it by hand, and it would take time but I was good with a needle and thread and had a beautiful top ready in a couple of days. I tried it on and loved it except it looked a little plain. I thought about it for a while and then decided to embroider something on the shoulder. I found embroidery floss in with my sewing supplies and started to work, not knowing what to make, thinking if I didn't like it I could rip out the stitches. Before long a white lotus blossom appeared. I followed it up with a couple of green leaves. I stood and admired it; this made all the difference in the world and decided to wear it with my new jeans when I went to my doctor's appointment.

THREE

I WAS IN A FOREST COVERED WITH TALL PINE TREES; ferns grew underneath the trees. It looked cold, but I was surprisingly warm. I looked up at the trees and suddenly knew I was not alone. I heard a rustle in the trees and then he was beside me. I looked around and then straight at him, into those blue/green eyes. He came closer, and his body was as beautiful as his eyes. We looked at each other for a while and then he came even closer to me. He put his arms around me and drew me tight to him and then his lips were on mine. He parted my lips with his tongue and his hand circled my waist and then slipped beneath my lotus blouse and. . . . .

"CHAN-LEI" I heard my name. "Chan-lei, wake up. I think you are dreaming. What are you dreaming about?" Chi said quietly. "You seemed to be moaning."

"Nothing," I whispered back. "I think it was about my doctor's appointment today." How could I dream such a thing? I loved Chi, how could I dream of another man?

I could never tell Chi what the dream was about? How could I tell him I was kissing another man? I would just have to push it out of my mind and not think about Eric O'Malley.

After Chi left for work, I dressed for the doctor. Jenny would be here in an hour. I took a shower and put on my new jeans. I slipped the lotus blouse over my head and looked in the mirror, I looked like an Asian American, I laughed to myself. I tidied up the kitchen, and before I knew it, Jenny was at the door.

She breezed in as if she had always been there, although this was the first time she had been in my apartment.

"Oh my," Jenny said, "what a darling apartment. I love the way you have decorated with the red pillows and other red accents. And Chan-lei, where did you get that adorable blouse? I love it, and I want one."

"I made it," I laughed. "My mother sent me fabric, and this is the first thing I made."

"Did you embroider the flower? What talent you have."

We talked for a few more minutes. I offered Jenny tea, but she said we had better get going; it would take a little while to get to her house. I put a jacket on, and we left the apartment. As we went through the store, Mrs. Ling gave me her usual sour look.

We walked down to Washington Street and waited for the cable car. I felt excited to ride on an actual cable car. Jenny told me to jump on without hesitation. I hung on to the pole. Very few people sat on cable cars; they hang on to the poles so they can jump off quickly. We went down Washington Street stopping many times. We got off on Fillmore Street and it was a quick couple of blocks to Jenny's house. It was amazing how everything changed, Pacific Heights was so different from Chinatown. The houses were big and Victorian. I had read about Victorian houses in San Francisco and it was exciting to be seeing them. When we reached Jenny's house, it was the most beautiful house I had ever seen. It was three stories tall. We entered into a foyer that was larger than my apartment, beautiful and decorated with gorgeous Chinese art, paintings on the wall, and a large teak table with a lamp.

A very pretty woman walked out to meet us. She had dark hair with a few streaks of gray. Her kind eyes were the first thing I noticed.

Jenny said, "This is my mother, Dr. Wu."

"Very pleased to meet you Chan-lei. Jenny has told me about you."

"Pleased to meet you too," I shook her hand.

I felt a little shy in front of her, she seemed to pick up on this and suggested we have tea before the examination.

We sat and talked, I told her of our voyage from China and how sick I had been on the ship, but now I was feeling much better, although a little tired at times.

Then she took me into her examining room. There was an examining table and a gown waiting there. I took off my jacket, and she looked at my new blouse.

"What a beautiful blouse," she said. "Did you buy it here or bring it from China?"

"I made it," I said rather shyly.

"Oh my, you have some talent, I know women who would pay dearly for something like *that*."

I smiled and thought it wasn't very special.

Dr. Wu left, I put the gown on and waited for her. She came back and was so gentle and sweet as she examined me. She asked me a lot of questions and wrote everything down.

"Well, I would say you are about eight weeks pregnant," she announced.

Tears came into my eyes, I was pregnant. I would be having a baby. I thought of how happy Chi would be, but I still worried.

She put something on my stomach she called a *Doppler*. It began to make a strange noise, and I heard a beating sound.

"Your baby's heart beating," she said gently.

"Really," I said, "that is her heart, not mine?"

"Don't get ahead of yourself," she laughed. "We don't know the sex of the baby yet."

"Oh, I know it is a girl," I said.

"We will see," is all she said.

Everything seemed to change inside me. Instead of feeling I wasn't ready for a baby I suddenly couldn't wait for her, feeling in my bones it was a girl.

"I want to see you again in four weeks," Dr. Wu said. "At that time I can do an ultrasound and we can see the baby."

"Oh my," I said.

"I don't have the equipment here," she said. "I can do it at the Chinese Hospital. Bring your husband and he can see the baby."

"I'm so excited, Dr. Wu, thank you so much." I said.

She gave me a bottle of vitamins and told me to start taking them, saying they would help with the fatigue.

After we left Jenny's home, I was so excited I could hardly stand it. Jenny suggested we go and have lunch somewhere. We found a charming little café near Jenny's house and went in.

We sat down, and looked around the room and there he was. The blue-eyed man sat just a table away with a couple of Asian men. I quickly looked away, but all their eyes seemed to be on me and Eric whispered something to the other men. They made me nervous, and I swore to myself not to even think about this man. After all, Chi and I were having a baby, we would be a real family. I loved my husband. *Why did this man affect me so much? And what was with that dream?*

After I returned home I was happy and excited, I didn't know what to do, all my feelings had changed. I sat in the chair next to the window and watched down the street for Chi to appear, walking home. It wasn't long before I saw him, looking so handsome and sweet, *I am lucky to have him as a husband. So why did I keep thinking about that silly dream and blue eyes?*

Chi came in the door carrying a takeout carton from the restaurant. It was so nice that he could bring food home. The restaurant was one of the best in San Francisco and the food delicious.

"Tell me about the doctor's visit," he said.

"Oh, Chi, we *are* having a baby. Dr. Wu is so nice, and I think she is a really good doctor. I got to hear the baby's heartbeat."

"So soon," Chi seemed surprised.

"Yes, she used a thing she called a Doppler, and I could hear the heartbeat all over the room. She said that next month she could do an ultrasound, and you can come with me so we can see the baby together. She told me I am about eight weeks pregnant and when she does the ultrasound we can watch the heart beating. Chi, I am so excited and happy."

"Oh, Chan-lei, we are going to be a real family." He gave me a big hug, and I don't think I had ever seen anyone look as happy as he did at that moment.

"I'm so happy we will raise our son in America," he said.

"What makes you think it is a son? A daughter would be very nice," I shot back.

In China, boys are considered to be best, girls are never given the honor boys receive. I would be happy with a baby boy, but in my heart I wanted a daughter. Now I worried that Chi would be disappointed with a girl.

"That is not what I meant, Chan-lei," Chi responded. "I would love a daughter just as much as a son."

"We will not be in China, Chi; we will be in America where girls are just as important as boys."

"Oh darling, I didn't mean it the way it sounded. I will love the baby the same whether it is a boy or a girl. I'm so sorry I made you feel otherwise."

As I set the table, I thought about Chi saying a son. I didn't know where I got the courage to say what I did about girls, I usually agreed with whatever Chi said. "Maybe America was rubbing off on me.

We ate the dinner Chi brought home and watched television the rest of the evening. We were happy that evening, but I still had the lingering thought that Chi would prefer a boy. The next day I was meeting Jenny to go shopping for maternity clothes, I would talk to her about it.

The next morning Jenny came over early. We had tea and talked before going shopping. She told me she was going to her school the next week to choose her classes for next semester. She suggested I go with her.

"You have seven months before the baby is born," Jenny said, "plenty of time for one semester. Why don't you come with me and meet with a counselor?"

I thought about it and decided I would do it. I wasn't sure if I would be accepted, but there was no harm in trying. I thought I would probably have to do a couple of semesters at the Community College before transferring to a University and I wasn't sure if they would accept my transcripts from China.

I decided to keep this a secret from Chi.

I didn't like any of the maternity clothes we looked at so I ended up just getting a pair of jeans a size larger and a couple of loose fitting shirts.

The following week I concentrated on the apartment and did a little sewing. I made a loose fitting dress out of the dark blue silk my mother had sent and ended up embroidering a lotus flower on it also. I didn't make the traditional Chinese dress; this dress was very simple and looked American. I wasn't sure where I would wear a dress like that, but there would be an occasion sometime, I was certain. Chi hadn't said anything about my jeans, but I felt he didn't approve.

One day I was in the Ling store buying a couple of items when I looked up and saw the blue-eyed man looking at me. I blushed, paid for my items quickly and went upstairs. *Why was he looking at me? Why did I think about him? What was wrong with me? I had everything, why would I think about this man?*

The next week I went with Jenny to San Francisco State University. I looked up at the big buildings, and my heart told me I wanted to study at this school. We went into the counselor's office, and Jenny explained that I could take a number and wait, and they would call me to talk to a counselor. I did just that, and Jenny said she would meet me back here, she was going to sign up for her classes. I sat down and before long I heard my number.

The counselor was a very nice man. I told him I had just arrived from China. He asked me questions about my education there, made some notes and told me he needed to get my transcripts and would call me.

Jenny didn't take long, and we went back to Chinatown. My head was full of thoughts; I was achieving my dreams even if I was hiding it. I was in America, expecting a baby and had a wonderful husband. I had made our drab little apartment into a real home. I wrote a long letter to my mother telling her of the doctor's visit, the University and everything else, except the blue-eyed man. Why was I still thinking about him? I told her I had not told Chi about the University, I was waiting for the good time and asked her not to say anything to Chi's parents. I would tell Chi when the time was right.

Shirley Nolan

FOUR

THE NEXT WEEK WAS QUIET. I DID SOME SEWING TO KEEP myself busy, I went to the public library and got my library card. I checked out a couple of English novels to improve my reading and writing of the language. I was not too bad at speaking English, but not sure about reading, and would need to read English if I intended on taking classes. Jenny came over once, but she was busy with school and finishing up her semester. Later in the week I received a call from a counselor at the University; she was very nice and had received my school records.

"Why didn't you tell us you were an honor student?" she said nicely.

I hadn't even thought of telling her that I was a very good student. She didn't think I would have any trouble being accepted for the next semester and told me to come in and fill out some forms and pick out my classes.

For the next hour I was walking on air. Everything was going so good it frightened me. I called Jenny, and we decided that we would meet at the University the following Wednesday. I felt I could find my way there by myself now. I thought about venturing out of Chinatown and exploring more of the city, I was feeling confident.

I was feeling good physically, no more nausea at all, and the tiredness was disappearing. I was happy and content. Time was dragging waiting for my next appointment with Dr. Wu and the sonogram. *Just think I will be able to see my baby,* I said to myself. I did have pangs of missing my parents, especially my mother, I wished their visas would come through soon. It was hard not to be able to talk to my mother. We did call at least once a week, although phone calls to China were expensive.

Chi was doing well at the restaurant and already received a raise. He enjoyed cooking there and had met some very nice people, he was happy. He felt it wouldn't be long until he would receive a promotion and even more money.

On Monday, I decided I would try to do some shopping on my own. I didn't want to shop in Chinatown, so I ventured into the city. Jenny had mentioned there were unusual and great shops on Union Street in downtown San Francisco. I dressed as American as possible, in a jeans and a T-shirt and headed out to catch the cable car and head downtown. It was a cold and damp day, so I wore my heaviest jacket, it was not all that warm, but would do. I was excited to be exploring on my own, my English was good enough I could get around with little trouble. Chi and I had studied English since we were small children, but spoke only Chinese at home in China. I was surprised when we started speaking English here, how fast it improved

When I reached Union Street, I was astonished at how different it was from Chinatown. The shops were glorious! I went into a baby shop, with beautiful baby clothes, and bought a lovely hand knit baby blanket that was on sale. I walked down the street looking in the windows and suddenly stopped! In one window was the most beautiful cradle I had ever seen; it was brass and in an oval shape. This was the perfect bed for my baby! I stood there for what seemed like hours just staring at it, I wanted it! I finally checked the price, $1,000.00! I knew it was too expensive, but I could figure out a way to save the money. I still had a lot of time before the baby arrived, I had to talk to Chi, I had to come up with something to earn money. I simply had to have it. I laughed to myself because it was the first tangible thing I had ever wanted that much. Usually, I could do without pricey items.

Next I found a maternity shop that had clothes I liked. I bought a couple of outfits but did not spend much money. I had to be frugal now that I had a goal to save for that gorgeous bed. It was a bit silly to want something that cost so much, but somehow I would find a way.

When I left the maternity shop, it had turned even colder. The San Francisco weather is always a little damp and cold, and when the wind blows off the bay, it seems like the cold goes right through a person, down to the bones. Also, the fog was rolling in. I shivered and started walking toward the cable car and was eager to get home. As I walked, I spotted a little shop with some very nice coats in the window and decided to go in and look. Within a few short minutes, I bought a new warm coat and a lovely scarf. Even though they were on sale and not that expensive, I thought to myself, "Well, there goes my budget." Next door was a little café, so I stopped in to have a warm cup of tea before heading home. I sat down at a small table and soon a very nice waitress came over.

"It is really cold out there today," she said. "What can I get for you?"

"I'm freezing," I said. "I just bought a new coat; maybe I should put it on," I laughed. And I will have a cup of tea."

"I think you should put the coat on," she laughed. I'll have the tea right out to you."

I took my new coat out of the bag and took off the tags. I took off my light coat and put it in the bag and put the new coat. I felt wonderful in it; it was the softest of soft wool, tan and had gorgeous brass buttons. I wrapped the red scarf around my neck, feeling so stylish! I drank my tea and left. Now I was extremely eager to get home.

When I stepped outside of the café, there was a soft mist falling with the fog and it had turned even colder. As I hurried toward the cable car, I saw him coming toward me, Eric with the blue eyes. He stopped in front of me.

"Don't I know you?" he said. "You are the girl that lives over the Ling's store."

"Yes," I stuttered. "My husband and I live there."

"I'm going up that way, it is freezing out here, can give you a ride?"

I didn't know what to say. I knew I shouldn't ride with him, but I didn't want to hurt his feelings.

"Okay," I finally managed to say.

"My car is right here." He walked over to a car parked by the curb. What a car! It was long and black; I had no idea what kind of a car it was.

He opened the door for me, and I got into black leather seats. I felt shy and couldn't say a word. I couldn't help but admire the luxury of the car, the seats were soft and comforting. I had never seen a car like this before. In China, there are very few cars. My parents have never owned a car, we got around with public transportation or on bicycles.

"How long have you been in the United States?" he asked me.

My voice returned, "Not long," I managed to say. "My husband and I came here only a few weeks ago."

"How do you like it so far?" he said.

"I love it! We have wanted to come to America since we were very young."

"You are still very young," he said as he seemed to look me up and down.

His look made me uncomfortable but at the same time I liked the idea that he looked at me like he admired my looks.

 It wasn't long before he pulled up in front of the little grocery store. I stammered a thank you and got out. He said goodbye and drove off.

When I went into the store, Mrs. Ling gave me a dirty look. I hurried up the stairs with my packages.

It wasn't long before Chi came in with a strange look on his face.

"Where have you been today?" he asked.

"I went downtown San Francisco to do some shopping. Oh, Chi, it was so cold I bought a new coat. I hope I didn't spend too much money."

Chi looked like he was angry with me. He never really got angry, but his look was one of anger.

"When I came in the store, Mrs. Ling stopped me and said you were out shopping all day *with the blue-eyed Chinese man.* She said you came in with lots of packages and were laughing, and it looked like you were having a good time with him."

"Oh Chi," I answered. "That is not true. Why does this lady hate me so much? I went downtown shopping quite alone, and it turned very cold. I was freezing, and Eric came walking along and offered me a ride home, I was with him no more than ten minutes,"

I couldn't believe that this evil woman had said those things. I showed Chi the blanket I had bought for the baby, the maternity clothes, and the coat and scarf. Only three packages, not a bunch of packages!

"Be careful who you ride with," Chi cautioned. "Eric O'Malley is probably alright, but I hear stories of people in Chinatown who should not be trusted."

"Jenny told me the same thing," I said seriously. "She even told me to watch out for Eric, I will be more careful from now on. But oh Chi you should see his car. It was big and black, and the seats were so soft. I have no idea how anyone could afford such a car. We may have a car someday but never one like his."

Chi came over and gave me a big hug and told me he was sorry he had believed Mrs. Ling, if only for a moment. It was then that I told him about the cradle I had seen. When I told him what it cost he took a deep breath.

"I want you to have whatever you want, but that is a little expensive. We will have to see what we can do. And I'm so sorry for believing anything Mrs. Ling would say," he said again. "I know you would not be out shopping with another man."

"Mrs. Ling seems to be such an unhappy woman; I wonder what made her the way she is?"

"I don't know Chan-lei; let's just forget about her for now. I'm sorry I was angry with you, I just worry about you."

I showed Chi my new coat again, and he thought it was nice and was happy that I had bought it. He told me I looked beautiful in it when I tried it on for him.

"It is lovely and will keep you and our little one warm," he said in Chinese. I hugged Chi and was happy that I had him and our baby growing inside me. But my thoughts also went to blue eyes and beautiful cars.

Shirley Nolan

FIVE

ON WEDNESDAY, I DRESSED IN MY FADED JEANS AND lotus shirt to go to the University. I was excited, and found the way without a problem, arriving a half-hour early to meet Jenny. We agreed to meet in the student lounge. As I sat and waited, I was both excited and nervous.

I saw Jenny walk in or I should say she danced in, Jenny had a way of walking that looked like a little fairy or a pixie. She never looks like she is walking, she floats on her feet. She looked adorable with her hair standing up in spots. I thought again about cutting my hair but I knew that Chi loved my long hair. My hair fell almost to my waist and it was thick and glossy. He would never like it short like Jenny's. My hair was distinct the way it was; like Jenny's was to her.

"Oh Chan-lei, I'm so glad to see you," Jenny gushed. "I've been so busy getting ready for finals that I haven't had a chance to come and visit you. How have you been?"

"I've been well, no more nausea, and I have a lot more energy than I did even a week ago. I'm so excited about today and I see your mother again a week from tomorrow. There is so much excitement going on in my life."

I seemed to gush as much as Jenny did, I wanted to tell her about the ride in that beautiful car but I thought better of it, I would tell her later.

We walked slowly over to the counselor offices. The University was beautiful, with green grass, picturesque little walks, and the buildings, oh my, the buildings were magnificent, I couldn't help but gawk at it all.

"Jenny, this campus stunning, it is hard to believe I'm going to be a student here."

Jenny laughed her lilting little laugh. I looked around at the students that were passing by. They were in all shapes, sizes, races and colors. I did notice quite a few Asian students, this made me feel comfortable, but honestly I couldn't wait to make friends from other cultures too.

The counselling office was nice but seemed a little small for a school this large, I went up to the little window and gave my name. It seemed like seconds before I heard my name being called. I looked at Jenny with nervousness.

"It will be fine," Jenny said. "I will wait for you and then we can go have lunch."

I followed the girl into the office.

"Mrs. Hammonds will be right in," she said kindly.

Mrs. Hammonds walked in about five minutes later. She looked to be about middle age, I would guess in her 50 or 60's. She was nice looking, probably a beauty when she was younger, but still good looking. She introduced herself and shook my hand. She went over my transcripts from China, explained to me I had very good grades but since I was new to America maybe I should start with a couple of the easier classes. Then she asked what I planned to study.

I had thought about this and almost decided on the arts, but all of sudden it popped out of my mouth, "*LAW,*" I said. What happened to all the thoughts I had about studying design and the arts? Law, where did that come from? Suddenly it all came to me, yes law, if I became an attorney maybe I could help other immigrants, in this wonderful country, become citizens and make the journey so much easier for them. I was shocked what I had said, but honestly it all made sense. I had thought about it before but thought it was impossible and I had better think of other careers such as the arts, I didn't think Chi would approve of law.

Mrs. Hammonds seemed a little surprised but she went right on offering me classes that would help me achieve my goal. She explained that I would have to become a citizen before I could take the Bar exam in California. No problem, I told her that is what I wanted and would begin that process as soon as possible. Then, I told her I was expecting a baby. Since my due date was June 14th she didn't think this would be a problem. The last week of the semester was in May. She also told me the University had an excellent day care center and the following semester I could bring my baby with me and leave her or him in the nursery while I was in classes. This was wonderful news.

Before I left I had chosen two classes, one in English and one in Math. I was on my way! My first semester would start on January 14th.

Jenny and I decided we would have lunch in the student center before I started home. The place was full to overflowing but we found a small table and sat down. I wasn't hungry so decided on a small salad. Jenny began to tell me about her finals and how hard they were and she had been doing nothing but studying.

"I took your advice about Union Street and went shopping there," I told her. "I bought this new coat and some baby things."

"I told you how nice that street is," Jenny said.

"I also found a brass cradle that I must have," I laughed.

"The coat is pretty," Jenny said, "Did you go alone?"

"Yes, but when I was leaving I ran into Eric O'Malley. He gave me a ride home in his car. Oh Jenny, his car is gorgeous."

Jenny looked at me kind of funny and then she gently said, "Chanlei, I told you to watch out for him. He seems nice, is good looking and has nice manners but I have heard rumors that he is in to all kinds of dangerous things."

"What kind of things?" I asked.

"I have heard rumors that he sells drugs, for example. There are even rumors that he deals in human trafficking."

"What is that?" I said with a shocked expression.

"Human trafficking is the slave trade. I've heard of people, especially young girls, disappearing. They say they are put on ships and sent to other countries and sold into prostitution."

I was shocked. I couldn't imagine Eric doing such a thing. He seemed so nice and he did have wonderful manners.

"Oh Jenny, you must be wrong," I said. "He was so nice and was only offering me a ride because it had turned so cold and foggy. His car was nice and warm and he took me right home."

"Be careful, Chan-lei. I feel he has reasons to be nice to you. Does he know you are married? Also does he know you are having a baby?"

"He knows I'm married," I laughed. "But no one knows about the baby except you and your mother, and now the counselor. Everyone will know soon enough." I put my hand on my stomach and could feel a small lump that was beginning to grow there. "I will be fat soon."

We changed the subject and talked about school, shopping, clothes and the cradle I wanted so much. I told Jenny I needed to find a way to earn the money for it. Also I confided in her I wanted to study law. I knew it would take much longer but I think that is what I want to do.

"Jenny." I said stuttering, "I haven't told Chi that I am going to the University. He is an old school type of man and I think he wants me to stay home and let him have the career."

"You know you will have to tell him eventually," Jenny said. "How did you meet Chi?"

"We were children together and our parents were friends. Our parents always wanted us to marry when we grew up. When I was 18 years old Chi asked me to marry him. It was not an arranged marriage with contracts and all but it was just understood. I loved Chi and thought he would make a good husband but I did not see fireworks like my friends had said."

"I totally understand Chan-lei," Jenny said. "But you do love him?"

"Oh yes, I do love him, he is a good man, but wish he understood how much I would like to have a career AND a happy family."

After lunch Jenny had to go to class and I started home. I was getting so good at getting around the city, at least to the places I knew but I took a wrong turn coming out of the University and I thought I was lost. The University was big and I stepped out on a street I didn't know and was all turned around. Finally, I found my way back to familiar ground and realized I didn't know everything and could get lost easily.

On my way home I noticed that the whole city was lit up with Christmas decorations. It was all so beautiful. In China people didn't celebrate Christmas. Only the Christians did, but not with decorations. I loved the way everything seemed to be decorated. Almost every door had a wreath hanging on it. And I saw decorated trees in the windows. Even the street lights were decorated. I made a note to myself to talk to Jenny about this. When I got into Chinatown I noticed for the first time that even the pagodas were decorated. Oh how I loved this country.

When I got home, I looked around the store for a few minutes, I needed tea and maybe something for a snack. It was warm in the store so I took my coat off and hung it over my arm. I wasn't hungry at lunch but now I felt I could use a snack. I found my favorite tea and then picked up a box of biscuits that looked good.

As I rounded a corner I dropped the biscuits and when I leaned down to pick them up I stood up and looked eye to eye with none other than Eric. His eyes seemed to burn into mine.

"Hello, Chan-lei," he said. "How are you today?"

"I'm fine," I stammered.

He seemed to look me up and down again and then said, "Where did you get that beautiful blouse you are wearing? I'm looking for something special for my mother for Christmas and this would be perfect."

"I didn't buy it, I made it," I said shyly.

"Would you consider making another one?" he said. I would pay for the materials and give you a hundred dollars for your trouble. It would have to be a little larger than yours; my mother is a bit heavier than you are."

I couldn't believe what I was hearing. A hundred dollars? I could put the money toward the cradle. I had some of the red silk left, hopefully enough to make a larger blouse.

"I think I could do that. I may have enough of the material left to make it. How much larger would it have to be?"

"Not much, my Mother is not large, but you are so tiny."

Again he seemed to look at me with those eyes like he admired me. I told him I would get started on it right away and should have it ready for him in about a week. He said he would check back then. Then he did a strange thing, he pushed my hair back from my face.

"You have beautiful hair," he said and smiled at me.

I went to pay for my purchases and Mrs. Ling gave me her usual sour look and then she said, "Be careful of that man Chan-lei. And you shouldn't be flirting; you are married to Chi aren't you?"

I was so surprised at her I couldn't even answer. I mumbled something like yes; I wasn't sure what I said. I wanted to get away from her

I went upstairs and made a cup of tea. I was now so nervous I wasn't hungry for the biscuits. It wasn't long before Chi came home. I told him about my day, having lunch with Jenny but I didn't tell him about the University. Instead I told him I was going to do some sewing for people and maybe take a sewing class or two. That would explain my absence when I was in classes. Poor Chi looked so tired. It was then that I realized how hard he was working. While he was working all the time I was running around having fun and now not telling him the truth.

"Don't you think you should take it a little easier, Chan-lei. I'm not sure you should be running around this city by yourself all the time, anything could happen to you."

I smiled at Chi. He was encouraging but he was a little worried. Chi was such a kind man but at the same time he was "old school" having been raised in a country where men were in control. He wanted me to do the things I wanted to a point, but he also wanted me to be his wife and a mother to his child.

"Oh Chi, I think I found a way to earn money for the cradle I want. I saw Eric O'Malley in the store and he wants me to make a blouse like this one for his mother. He said he would pay me a hundred dollars. That would only leave nine hundred more for me to earn," I laughed.

"That is good, but we will find a way to buy that cradle, you don't have to work for it. It is for our child; I could work overtime at the restaurant."

"But Chi, you work so hard already. I think I should help out more. We will also have other expenses."

Then I told him what Mrs. Ling had said and that she had accused me of flirting with Eric.

"I don't think he is dangerous Chi, he is always so nice to me and he has such good manners. Mrs. Ling is wrong about me flirting with him so I feel she is wrong about him being involved in dangerous activities."

I didn't tell him that Jenny had also warned me about Eric.

Chi looked skeptical and I realized Chi had never met Eric. He hadn't even noticed him that first day in the store.

SIX

I WOKE UP EARLY; A FAINT LIGHT WAS COMING IN through the window. Chi was asleep next to me. Looking over at him, he looked so sweet and kind. *He is a handsome man,* I thought to myself. *Any woman would be lucky to have him as her husband. He works hard and gives me most anything I want. I'm being selfish,* I thought. *I've been running all over the city by myself and spending money that Chi works so hard for. I've only been thinking of myself. I have feelings about Eric who is charming and exotic. What is wrong with me? I have a husband that is kind to me. So what if he is traditional and wants me to be a wife and mother, I shouldn't lie to him about school.* I thought about when we were children in China. Chi always played games with me and I usually won. Did he lose on purpose? I knew he always loved me. Our parents were best friends; they were so happy when we married. I missed my family so much. *If only my mother was here to talk to.* I decided I would call her today, but then I thought about the money and the long distance bill. Maybe I would wait. Chi stirred beside me and I thought I was going to change. I would do nice little things for him. I would love him more and not think about blue eyes.

The lotus blouse was finished, pressed and hanging on a hanger. I had taken extra care to make it perfect, even the lotus embroidery was so much better than my blouse. I spent the morning cleaning and making the apartment look pretty. I wanted to call my mother but then thought better of it again. I would wait until after my appointment with Dr. Wu.

Eric left a message with Mr. Ling to meet him around noon to give him the blouse. I felt nervous and didn't know why. Give him the blouse and be done with it. *Don't look at those blue eyes.*

I waited until about ten minutes after noon; I took the blouse and headed down. When I walked into the store, Mrs. Ling looked at me and the blouse and then said, "There is someone waiting for you Chan-lei," giving me one of her disapproving looks.

Eric walked up to me. "I see you finished the blouse," he said looking at me with his sultry eyes.

"Oh yes, here it is, I hope you like it. If it's not the right size I will make another." I said as I handed it to him.

He looked at the blouse and then said, "I think it is perfect. So perfect, if my mother wants another, will you be willing to make it?"

"Of course," I said "But if she doesn't like this one I can do another." I repeated myself.

"That won't be necessary," he said.

He took two one hundred dollar bills out of his wallet and handed them to me.

"I thought you said one hundred dollars," I said.

"Yes, but that didn't include the materials," he said looking at me with those smoldering eyes.

"I already had the materials," I said. "One hundred dollars is too much."

"Your talent is amazing," he said. This blouse is worth much more; I insist that you take it."

I didn't argue with him. He gave me another one of his looks, looking me up and down and then was gone. Mrs. Ling was watching the entire event, she had a strange smile on her lips.

I went back up to my apartment. *Two hundred dollars*, I thought to myself. I guess it is alright, he seems to have a lot of money, but two hundred dollars seems way too much.

A while later Chi came home. He had had an early start at work this morning so he came home early. I was excited to tell him about the two hundred dollars. I noticed he had a small paper bag with him. He took a little black lacquered box out of the bag. It was the kind that was sold in every shop in Chinatown with little Chinese symbols and flowers painted on it. This one had a lotus flower. I didn't know if Chi picked it because of the lotus or it was by chance.

"What is this?" I asked.

"I was thinking about the cradle today at work and I thought we could save money in this little box. You know, I get tips at the restaurant once in a while, not always, but sometimes customers like to tip the chefs. I usually mix this in with our other money. But I think if we keep it separate, it might add up pretty fast. What do you think?"

"Oh Chi, that is a wonderful idea," I said excitedly. "And today I earned two hundred dollars for the blouse I made, so we can put that in it first."

"Two hundred dollars! I thought you were going to get one hundred dollars for your sewing."

"That was the agreement, but Eric insisted on paying me two hundred instead of one hundred. He said it was for the materials, but the materials didn't cost me anything; it was the silk my mother sent."

Chi was surprised. I took out the money and we put it in the box. Chi placed the box on a high shelf. It looked so pretty sitting up there. I knew that there were boxes like this in every shop but this one was special.

I looked at him and thought how sweet and caring he was. Even though the cradle was more than we could afford he was finding a way that we could have it. I did love him so much, I wished that my heart would beat faster when I saw him like it did when I saw Eric.

After dinner we watched our favorite show on television, *Family Ties*. We both thought that watching television improved our English. I loved this show and the interaction of the family. We watched several shows on television but already I had picked this one.

The characters were funny and all different from each other. Someday I wanted a house and more children, but first, let's start with this one, I smiled to myself.

The next day we walked the five blocks to the Chinese Hospital. Chi had taken the entire day off. He had talked to me the night before about spending some time in the city after my appointment.

"Maybe you can take me to see this wonderful cradle," he said with a smile.

"Oh Chi, that would be fun. Maybe we can have lunch or something."

"I was thinking we could go to Golden Gate Park; I hear it is beautiful. We haven't spent a day together since we left China," he laughed.

I thought again about how selfish I had been. I spent time doing everything for me and spending time with Jenny when I could, not Chi.

As we approached the hospital we could see there was a new modern entrance to the hospital but next to it was the old entrance complete with a pagoda. We entered and gave my name to the receptionist who told us to have a seat; someone would be with us soon. She gave me a paper to fill out. Noticing the paper was in both English and Chinese, I chose to fill it out in English.

It was only a few minutes when Dr. Wu walked up to us.

"Chan-lei, it is so good to see you," she said.

"Dr. Wu, this is my husband Chi." I didn't forget my manners.

Chi shook hands with Dr. Wu and then we walked down the hall to another room. The room looked strange with a lot of equipment. I was feeling nervous, my heart started to pound. A young lady, wearing a white lab coat, gave us a gentle smile.

"This is Sarah, she is the technician that will do the sonogram," Dr. Wu said. "Sit down here on the table and we will get started."

I sat on the table. It had paper on it and felt a bit uncomfortable. I leaned back on the pillows and was practically sitting up. Sarah told me to raise my shirt up. She had some kind of a strange thing in her hand that looked like a wand. There was also a big machine with a monitor that looked like a television set. She applied a gel to the wand and told me that it would be cold on my skin. It was cold, and she started to move it around on my stomach.

Sarah told me to look at the monitor. Dr. Wu was standing next to me and she told Chi to stand closer so he could see. I heard a strange whooshing sound like water rushing or something. The monitor had gray lines on it. Then I heard a beating sound.

"The sound you hear is the sound inside your uterus and the beating sound is your baby's heart," Sarah said. "A strong heart," she smiled. "Look at where I'm pointing." She had some little pointer thing like a pencil or something in her hand. "That is your baby's heart." I could see something dark and it was pulsing. "Now look here," she moved the pointer. "That is the head."

I was not sure what I was seeing but then I saw it, a tiny little head.

There was a real baby in there! Tears stung my eyes... *This is my baby!* I looked over at Chi and he had a tear in his eye. He looked amazed and I rethought my thought, this is *our* baby. Sarah moved the wand around on my stomach and began taking pictures or something, it was all so confusing. She showed us little arms and legs and even tiny hands.

"The baby is too small and turned the wrong way so I can't see if you have a boy or a girl, but all the measurements show a healthy baby. It is difficult to tell sometimes, even if you can see at this stage of pregnancy," Sarah said with a sorry sound to her voice. Suddenly I didn't care if it was a boy or a girl. *This was our baby!*

"That's okay Sarah," I said, "It doesn't matter, we will be surprised."

After she was finished and cleaned the gel off my stomach she handed me a picture. It was our baby's first picture. I was so excited, I felt like I couldn't breathe and I couldn't take my eyes off that picture.

There is an actual baby!

"Everything looks wonderful," Dr. Wu said. "Call and make an appointment in four weeks, I can see you at my house. There is no need to come to the hospital. We will not do another sonogram as long as everything seems to be okay."

We didn't need to check with the desk. Dr. Wu said the insurance would take care of the cost and if there was more they would send us a bill. Chi had taken out health insurance with his work but we had been afraid that it would not pay since I was already pregnant at the time but Dr. Wu said the hospital had checked with the insurance company and it was all fine. I also reminded Dr. Wu to send me a bill for her services; I had not received one yet for the office visit at her house. She smiled and said she would mention it to her office manager.

I thanked both Dr. Wu and Sarah. Then Chi thanked them again and again. We left the hospital and walked down to catch the cable car. Chi suggested we go to the shop were the cradle was first. I kept sneaking looks at the photo of our baby. As we were waiting for the cable car, a big black car passed by.

No, I thought, it can't be.

At the baby shop, Chi was as impressed with the cradle as I had been. He said he could imagine our little baby sleeping in it. Then we looked at bedding for the cradle. Since we didn't know, well he didn't know, if the baby was a boy or a girl, we decided on a light green set with panda bears and bamboo appliqued on the blanket and the little pillow. It looked like home in China to us, and would work for a boy or a girl. The shopkeeper assured us they always had that set and if not they could order it and have it there in a couple of days, so we decided to wait and buy it when we bought the cradle.

We were both hungry so we went into a little café for lunch. It was warm and pleasant and we kept looking at the picture of our baby. As we were leaving I saw a big black car driving slowly up the street. *Don't even think it,* I told myself.

"Now that you have a picture of our baby maybe you will stop thinking about a career and focus on the baby and my career," Chi said.

I grew defensive and came back with, "I don't understand why I can't do both."

"Chan-lei, I am the head of this family and will decide what we will have and not have."

I stopped talking. I was happy I hadn't told Chi about my classes. I would have to do this on my own.

Next we found another little shop and bought a picture frame to put our "baby" in and headed toward the park.

When we got to Golden Gate Park we were amazed at how big and beautiful it was. It had also turned cold. I had my warm coat and scarf but Chi was wearing only a light jacket. We found the duck pond and fed the ducks for a while and decided we should go home to hot tea and the warmth of our apartment. Besides my mood was somber and I wanted to go home. I wasn't mad, just disappointed at Chi's attitude.

All the way home we kept looking at the beautiful Christmas decorations. Chi said he thought we should buy a little Christmas tree for the apartment. I wasn't so sure, thinking we shouldn't spend the money but it would be nice. In China, the state frowned on religion of any kind and most people did not celebrate Christmas at all. My parents were Christian, and we always had a little celebration. My mother would cook a special dinner, usually a duck, and we would have one present. My mother said that we had to have a small celebration and not let the birth of Jesus go unnoticed, but we never had a tree or any other decorations.

As we arrived home I thought I saw the black car again but told myself I was being silly. We went up to the apartment and Chi began to brew some tea.

"Chan-lei, why don't you run down to the store and get some of those cookies we like so much. This has been a special day for us and we need to celebrate a little," Chi said sounding so happy.

I went to the store and as I was picking up the cookies I turned around and looked into blue eyes.

"Hello, Chan-lei, how are you today?" he said with his sultry voice.

"I'm fine," I mumbled.

"The blouse you made is exquisite," he said. "My mother is going to love it. I can't think of a better present for her."

I had no idea what "exquisite" meant but it had to be good.

I said good-bye and thank you and then hurried to pay for the cookies and practically ran upstairs.

Chi had the tea ready and we had our tea and cookies and put our "baby" into the frame. We put the framed photo on the shelf in the living room. It looked so pretty, although you could hardly see it was a baby but Chi and I knew what it was.

Chi suggested that we call our parents. I called my mother first. She was happy to hear our news but was a bit confused as how we could see the baby inside of me. They did not have sonograms when she was expecting me. We talked about how we hoped they would be in America before the baby was born. We had until June, so there was still plenty of time. I wanted them to be here now, I missed my mother and father so much.

When Chi talked to his mother he had a look of concern on his face. He too told his mother that we hoped they would be here before the baby was born. After he hung up he told me his mother was worried about his father.

"He has been extremely tired lately and not feeling well at all. They are going to see the doctor as soon as possible," he said.

We settled into our evening and tried not to worry. It had been a special day even with Chi's attitude.

I would only think happy thoughts tonight, and keep my secret of school. Especially not think about blue-eyed Chinese men!

SEVEN

I WANTED TO DO SOMETHING SPECIAL FOR CHI BUT I was not sure what. I felt guilty about keeping things from him. It would be Christmas soon; maybe I could make him something, but what? He had been so sweet and the emotion he had shown when he saw the sonogram had touched my heart. He had brought home his tips and put them in the box but we decided only to count the money once a week. We were surprised when we realized we had almost four hundred dollars.

Jenny was finished with her exams and had stopped by to tell me that her mother wanted Chi and I to come over for Christmas dinner. We bought a tiny little tree and some decorations. We decided that every year we would add to the decorations. By the time our baby was a teenager we should have quite a wonderfully decorated house, we laughed. We were having such a good time together that I hardly thought of Eric but also was keeping my school plans hidden.

I was watching a morning game show on TV when Mr. Ling came to the door with a big box from my mother.

"Chan-lei, the postman just left this for you. My, the apartment looks so good, it has never looked so nice."

"Thank you Mr. Ling, I'm so happy you like it."

I hoped he would say something to Mrs. Ling. I closed the door and felt happy.

Opening the box I could not believe my eyes. My wonderful mother had sent me all kinds of fabric for baby clothes, soft yarns, and even knitting needles. Also the box contained baby clothes, some she had made and some were purchased, and more silk fabric, a light green the same shade as the bedding we picked out. I sat down on the floor and cried, I missed her so much. Looking at the green silk I thought it would be perfect for a shirt for Chi. This could be my special gift to him, and I should have enough of the fabric left to make something for the baby.

I cleared out one of my drawers in our dresser and put the new baby clothes in it. We needed another small dresser for the baby but I was not sure where we would put it.

That afternoon I walked down to the fabric store and bought a pattern for Chi's shirt and found a couple of knitting books for baby clothes. Feeling happy as I walked back home, I seemed to smile at every passerby. As I was entering the store a black car drove past. No, I thought! I decided I was being silly, there must be hundreds of big black cars in this city, and not every black car I saw was Eric's.

Before Chi returned home that afternoon I had the shirt cut out and almost basted together. I put it away in one of my dresser drawers where Chi would never find it. I felt pride for myself that I could sew and I was sure Chi would like the shirt. I cooked us a simple dinner and soon Chi came in the door.

I showed Chi the baby clothes my mother had sent. Chi commented on how small they were.

The next morning Jenny called and wanted to know if I was free for lunch. I was, I had nothing else to do but work on Chi's gift. I wanted to stay home and work on it but I said yes. We decided to meet at the University so I could price my textbooks in the bookstore. My financial aid had been approved and I was keeping that a secret from Chi also. I would have to tell him before long however, I didn't like feeling guilty.

I changed my clothes and noticed that everything was feeling a little tight. I had a difficult time buttoning my pants. *Oh my*, I thought, *I guess I'm going to have to start wearing the maternity pants I bought.*

Jenny was waiting for me at the bookstore. The books were not as expensive as I thought they would be and Jenny assured me that financial aid would pay for them anyway.

"How are you feeling?" Jenny asked.

"I feel great," I told her. I saw your mother the other day when I had my sonogram. Wow, that was something."

"I know," Jenny answered. "I've watched a couple of them with my mother. It is amazing to see a little baby in there."

"Chi and I both cried. They gave us a picture, we framed it."

Jenny laughed and I felt a little silly, but I treasured that picture.

We decided not to eat at the University and rode the cable car downtown. Jenny knew a cute little café there she wanted to go to.

We found a table and ordered. I was not very hungry but thought I had better eat for the baby, so I had a bowl of soup and some crackers.

"Are you coming to my house for Christmas?" Jenny asked. "My mother does Christmas well."

"Yes, thank you so much. What should we bring?"

"Just bring yourselves, there will be plenty of food."

We sat there for a little while and I told Jenny about the baby clothes and she talked about her classes and how she was afraid she had messed up one of her exams. She also told me about a boy she had met.

I told Jenny about the voyage to America and how sick I had been on the ship. I also told her how amazing it was when we arrived in San Francisco.

"I couldn't believe how beautiful the sea looked, all blue with a little green thrown in. I looked at the land and it was beautiful; but the sight that caught my eye was the golden bridge sticking out of the water above the fog. It was the most beautiful sight I had ever seen. I stood there amazed and Chi told me it was the Golden Gate."

"San Francisco is an amazing city, Chan-lei, full of opportunities," Jenny said.

"I may not be able to take advantage of those opportunities Jenny," I said sadly. "Chi seems to think I should be content to stay at home with the baby."

"We will change his mind," she said.

"I don't know; I haven't told him I'm going to take classes."

"I think you should tell him. Chan-lei, you have to stand up for yourself at some point. You deserve your dreams as much as he deserves his."

"We will see," I said meekly.

As we left the café I thought I saw a black car but dismissed it as being silly again.

When I got home Eric was in the store talking to Mrs. Ling. They seemed to be having a serious talk. I started to walk by them and Eric suddenly put his hand on my shoulder.

"Not talking to me Chan-lei?" he said.

"Oh, I didn't mean to be rude," I said. "I didn't want to interrupt you and Mrs. Ling." My stomach seemed to lurch when he touched me.

"It's okay," he said with a slight grin. "You can interrupt me anytime."

I didn't know what to think of that so I said polite hellos and hurried up to my apartment. I felt nervous and couldn't settle down all afternoon, I did a little more on the shirt, decided on a pattern to knit a baby blanket, and then put it all away and watched television until Chi came home. I couldn't keep my mind on anything. I looked at the picture of the baby again and again which seemed to be the only thing that calmed me.

The next day I felt much calmer and finished the shirt. I pressed it and then I noticed it looked a little plain so I took out my embroidery yarns and embroidered a tiny little lotus flower on the pocket. It looked nice, not feminine at all. Then I thought that I should take a gift to Jenny and her parents, but what?

Jenny had admired my lotus blouse; maybe I could make her one like it? I went through my materials and found a pretty jade silk that would be perfect for her. I spent the rest of the afternoon sewing on the blouse and before I knew it, it was time for Chi to come home.

The following day I finished Jenny's blouse and went down to the store to buy wrapping paper for both Chi and Jenny's presents. I noticed that Mrs. Ling was not in the store and felt relieved. I paid Mr. Ling for the paper and he was polite as usual. He said Mrs. Ling was out Christmas shopping.

When I went back upstairs I noticed there was an envelope stuck in the door. I picked it up and went inside. When I opened it, I was shocked and I'm sure I went as pale as a ghost. It was written in Chinese and said:

小心有蓝眼睛的人

When translated it said BE CAREFUL OF MEN WITH BLUE EYES!

I could hardly breathe; I sat down on the couch shaking, feeling a sick lump in my stomach. Who had left this note? Did Mrs. Ling sneak up here and leave it? But how could she? Mr. Ling had said she had gone downtown to do some Christmas shopping. Who had been up here at my door?

I was so nervous I could hardly stand it. I checked to make sure the door was locked over and over again. I paced throughout the apartment. I made some tea and my hands were shaking so much I almost dropped the cup. I made myself sit down and relax, but it was next to impossible. Finally, I got the shirt and blouse and wrapped them. I was afraid to turn on the television because I couldn't hear anyone lurking around my door.

Finally, I started to calm down. I took the note and hid it deep in one of my dresser drawers. I thought about telling Chi but decided against it, thinking it would only worry him. Who was trying to warn me about Eric? Did they think I was in physical danger or did they think Eric *liked* me too much? I wished my mother were here. I missed her and suddenly I even missed China. Things were so different in this new place. I loved it, but I missed the old way too. And now I had another secret I was keeping.

It wasn't long before Chi came in carrying a big box all wrapped in Christmas wrap. I was calm now and had decided maybe this note thing was a joke by someone. I also promised myself I would definitely avoid Eric as much as possible.

"What is this?" I asked Chi.

"It's your Christmas present," he answered with a smile. "And don't worry I didn't spend the cradle money."

We both laughed and Chi put the present under the tree. As he did he noticed my wrapped presents there.

"What are these?" He said.

"There is a present there for you and one for Jenny," I said, "and don't worry I didn't spend the cradle money."

We both laughed. I thought we could take Dr. Wu some flowers, she would like that. I told him about the blouse I had made for Jenny. He seemed unusually pleased for some reason.

I didn't mention the note to Chi. I tried hard to forget about it all together. It was probably like I thought; a prank from someone who saw me talking with Eric.

On Christmas Eve, Chi and I had our usual dinner and spent the evening watching TV. We didn't realize that a lot of people celebrated Christmas Eve as much as they celebrated Christmas Day. We sat down and watched television. I was sitting next to Chi on our small sofa when I felt a strange feeling in my stomach.

It felt almost like a butterfly was fluttering. I looked at Chi and he was concentrating on the television program.

"Chi," I said. "I feel something strange, like butterflies in my stomach. Do you think it could be the baby? Dr. Wu did say I should feel something soon."

Chi reached over and put his hand on my stomach. "I don't feel anything," he said.

"I don't think you could, it is faint but I think it is our baby,"

We looked into each other eyes and we both felt emotional. We both had tears.

The next morning, I slipped out of bed early and went into the kitchen and quietly prepared breakfast. As I looked around the apartment I was excited to think that this was our first Christmas, first Christmas together married and first Christmas that we could openly celebrate. I thought next year would be wonderful with the baby to celebrate with us. I tried not to think about the note but that was almost next to impossible. I wondered again who was warning me about Eric and why?

I cooked a special breakfast of bacon and eggs, and set the little table to look extra pretty. Very American! I was finishing up when Chi came in from the bedroom. When he saw the table he looked so pleased. At that moment I thought I felt the flutter again". We had breakfast and then decided to open our presents. Chi opened his first and looked so happy with the shirt.

"Oh Chan-lei, did you make this for me?"

"Of course," I said with glee. "Do you like it?"

"Like it, I love it. I can hardly wait to wear it. I will wear it today when we go to Dr. Wu's home."

Next I opened the large box Chi had for me. I gasped when I saw what it was.

"Chi, I can't believe it! A sewing machine!"

"You seem to be doing so much sewing lately and with the baby and all I thought this would be so much faster and easier for you. It was not expensive; one day I will buy you a much better one. See, Chan-lei, you will find lots of things to do at home."

My mood changed but I hugged him and gave him a kiss.

What a wonderful man, he gave me everything. He made me happy, but why couldn't he understand my dreams?

We spent most of day enjoying being together and I checked out everything about the new sewing machine. I could hardly wait to use it. I would start with a baby dress.

Later in the afternoon we dressed to go to the Wu's home. I wore the blue silk dress I had made and not worn yet. It fit well and was still loose enough that I could wear it much longer if there was an occasion. Chi looked wonderful in his new shirt. We stopped by a flower mart that was open and purchased a large poinsettia plant for Dr. Wu.

Jenny met us at the door and when we stepped into the house I held my breath. I could smell all kinds of delicious smells. The house was a Christmas wonderland. There were wreaths, swags, a nativity scene set up in the entry way. Since I had not seen many decorations any would have been beautiful, but these were exceptional. Jenny took the plant we had brought and was thrilled that I had brought her a gift as well.

"Oh Jenny, the house is so beautiful and it smells so good," I said.

"I told you my mother goes over the top! Come on and I will introduce you to everyone."

We met Jenny's aunt and uncle and a few friends that were there. It was a small group only about eight people. We went in the kitchen and Dr. Wu was there cooking. I thought it delightful that this busy doctor would be cooking Christmas dinner. She had it all, a family, beautiful home and a career. Standing beside her was a handsome older man.

Chan-lei, Chi, I would like you to meet my father, Charles Wu." Jenny introduced us.

We made some small talk and I told Dr. Wu I thought I had felt the baby. She was sure that was what it was. Then it was time to sit down to dinner.

The dining room table was spectacular. It was long and had tiny little Christmas trees at every place setting. The food was overflowing on the table. There was turkey, beef, duck and even a ham. The side dishes and the bread looked amazing. And everything tasted as good as it looked.

After dinner most of the guests left. Dr. Wu asked us to stay for a while. I offered to help her clean up but she said she had someone coming in later to do the clean-up.

"I do all the cooking but I like help cleaning up," she laughed.

We sat down in the living room and Dr. Wu served us tea with the daintiest little cakes. I was already so full I was ready to burst, but I couldn't resist the cakes. They were light and seemed to melt in your mouth. It was all so pleasant, the Christmas tree was huge and the decorations wonderful. This is Christmas in America, I felt overwhelmed by it all.

Jenny opened her present and was thrilled with the blouse.

"My favorite color," she said.

And she handed me a brightly decorated box.

"Oh Jenny," I said "You didn't need to get me anything."

"It is not so much for you," she teased.

I opened the box, being careful not to tear the paper. Inside was the most delicate baby blanket I had ever seen. I was thrilled, tears came to my eyes.

Dr. Wu talked about the baby and how she had hospital privileges in several of the San Francisco hospitals but she thought I would be most comfortable at the Chinese Hospital.

"Although you speak English," she said "most of the doctors and nurses also speak Chinese and there might be some things you don't understand as well in English."

How insightful of this woman. I agreed with her completely. Then I asked Mr. Wu what he did.

"I'm a lawyer," he said. "I'm an Assistant District Attorney for San

Francisco, in charge of the major crimes unit."

He went on to explain that he had District Attorneys under him and prosecuted the major crimes such as murder cases.

"Jenny here wants to follow in my footsteps," he said proudly.

Suddenly I blurted out, "I do too."

Chi gave me a harsh look.

I laughed, what was I thinking? I had thought of becoming a lawyer to work in immigration but was that what I wanted?

"Just kidding," I said, "But I would love to hear about your cases."

Well they are normally unsurprising," Mr. Wu said. "But there is one right now that my investigators and the San Francisco Police Department are working on that is anything but normal. There have not been any arrests as of yet."

"Can you talk about it?" I asked.

"Sure. It is one that we are having a great deal of problems finding any evidence to tie anyone to the crime. It seems that in the last five years, six young girls have gone missing. No trace of them whatsoever, they vanished. The one thing in common is they are all Asian, young and pretty. None of these girls were involved in anything sinister, in other words they were all good girls, going about their lives, going to school, working and just living. We are so afraid that they have been abducted into the slave trade. I have a suspect; I can't find enough on this person as yet to prosecute."

"Jenny told me about the slave trade," I said. "It is scary, I never realized such things exist."

"Be careful down in Chinatown," he said. "You are young and pretty. It is good that you are married and expecting a child. I'm glad you have Chi to protect you."

We talked for a while longer and then it was time for Chi and I to go home. I liked Mr. Wu. On the way home I thought about what he had said and also who was trying to warn me about Eric. I still didn't say anything to Chi about the note.

EIGHT

IN THE WEEK BETWEEN CHRISTMAS AND NEW YEAR'S, I barely left the apartment. I was so thrilled over my new sewing machine that all I wanted to do was sew. I set it up on the kitchen table every morning as soon as Chi left for work. I made a baby dress out of the left over green silk. *If the baby turns out to be a boy, I will save it because one day I will have a daughter*, I told myself. I embroidered little daisies on the yoke and was happy with the way it turned out. I also started knitting a baby blanket out of a soft yellow yarn that my mother had sent.

The baby blanket the Wu's had given us for Christmas was gorgeous. I took it out and looked at it several times a day, imagining how beautiful it would look in the cradle. On Friday night we took the box down and counted the money, five hundred and six dollars! It was adding up fast, we already had half of what we needed.

I thought a lot about what Mr. Wu had said about the slave trade. Who did he have in mind? I hoped it wasn't Eric. How could it be Eric? He was always so nice and polite; how could he be a criminal? I also thought about going to law school, but first I had to get through the University and get my bachelor's degree. I would be starting my classes in two weeks. I was so eager to get started. Both my classes met on Tuesdays and Thursdays, so I only had to make the trip to the University twice a week. It would be easy to explain my absence to Chi. I would tell him I was taking some advanced sewing classes.

I felt the baby every day now and it was getting stronger, and also noticed that I had a distinct belly, not big yet, but my stomach was not flat anymore. I decided to start wearing my maternity jeans. When I put them on they were so comfortable, so much more than my tight jeans.

On New Year's Eve, I went down to the store to get a few grocery items. I was wearing my jeans and a big shirt. Mrs. Ling looked me up and down and then said rather rudely, "Oh no, not a squalling brat upstairs."

Everything in my entire being bristled!

"My baby will not be a squalling brat," I said. "My baby will be a sweet baby that is loved much."

I turned around to leave and bumped into Eric. I was angry and he was the last person I wanted to see at the moment.

"Excuse me," I said politely. I was planning to walk down the street to another market close by.

"Chan-lei," he said kindly. "My mother loved the blouse you made and wondered if you would be able to do some more sewing for her."

"I don't believe so," I said, nicer than I felt. "I don't have the time right now, maybe later on, I'm sorry."

"I'm sorry too," he said "My mother will be disappointed."

I wanted to get away. I didn't want to talk to him and I wanted to get away from Mrs. Ling. How dare her say unkind things about my baby! Also I was not so sure about Eric, now he wants me to be a seamstress for his mother? *Wait until I am a successful lawyer*, I thought to myself.

"I need to get going," I muttered. "I have some errands to run."

I left the store as quickly as I could, and walked to a larger store down the street and bought the items I wanted. Maybe I wouldn't shop in the little store anymore. I spent some time looking through a couple more shops, hoping Eric would be gone and Mrs. Ling would be busy when I had to go through the store. I calmed down and was feeling better, but they were talking at the cash register when I came back.

I said a polite greeting and hurried toward the stairs, thinking I heard Mrs. Ling say something like "two for the price of one" and laugh when I walked by.

I guess they were talking about some item for sale.

I went upstairs and locked my door. The anger returned and tears started to sting my eyes, I wanted my mother. I thought about calling Jenny but decided against it. I put my groceries away and then sat down and knitted on the baby's blanket, but I was so agitated and nervous that I was afraid I would make a mistake so I put it away and made a cup of tea to calm myself. I thought about

Eric and I wasn't sure how I felt about him. Was he the kind man I thought he was? I was so confused. I would try to avoid him as much as possible. I have a lot more things to think about, my baby, school and Chi! And keeping secrets from Chi!

By the time Chi came home, I was calm. He brought home some treats from the restaurant; it was New Year's Eve. We had a nice meal and then watched TV until the New Year arrived. I told him about what Mrs. Ling had said and started to cry again. We both agreed that we wouldn't tolerate anyone speaking badly about our baby.

"Maybe we should look for another apartment as soon as the six months paid rent is up," Chi said. "Maybe outside of Chinatown, I was a little freaked out about what Mr. Wu said the other night. Hey, I'm using American slang like freaked out," he laughed.

We both laughed at this, feeling we were becoming Americans.

I had to admit I was a little *freaked out* too. I would love to live outside of Chinatown. I would love to live in Pacific Heights where the Wu's lived, but I knew that we couldn't afford anything there.

"Maybe somewhere close to Pacific Heights?" I suggested. "Can we start looking around now?"

"I'll ask around the restaurant," Chi said. "A lot of people come in there, they may know of something. I don't want you living around Mrs. Ling and her nasty comments."

The rent was paid until April so we would have to be careful until then. I felt happy that maybe we could find something else before the baby was born and be all moved in and away from Chinatown and Mrs. Ling. I would have to endure Mrs. Ling's remarks until then. I would stay as busy as possible and that would make the time pass quickly.

Before I knew it, it was time to start classes. I met Jenny a few days before at the bookstore and purchased my books with money I saved from my grocery money. I hid them in the bottom drawer of the dresser, where the note was hiding. I was getting good at deception, I thought sadly. I was feeling nervous about the first day of class and there was no hiding the fact that I was pregnant now. Mrs. Ling had not made any more comments, but I had avoided her as much as possible. I ran into Eric a few times in the store, but I was avoiding him too.

The first day of classes went well, everyone seemed nice and no one said anything about the fact I was pregnant. In fact, I saw several other pregnant students. I quickly fell into a routine, on Tuesdays and Thursdays I took the cable car to the University. I had to be there by 10:00AM and I was finished by 4:00PM so I was home by 5:00-5:30PM. Usually I met Jenny in the cafeteria for lunch. I had also met a couple of other students that would join us. On the days I didn't go to school, I did my homework as soon as Chi left for work, which was easy, and made baby clothes.

I saw Dr. Wu once a month. Everything was going perfect with my pregnancy. The baby was getting bigger and stronger. I could feel definite kicks and punches now. One evening I told Chi to put his hand on my stomach and he felt the baby moving. He was excited and asked if it hurt.

"No, it feels wonderful," I said. "It's hard to describe, but it is an amazing feeling."

I talked to my mother and she was upset because they still didn't have their visas. She also told me they were worried about Chi's father; he was not looking good at all. Mrs. Wah was worried about him too. Oh, how I hoped they would all be here soon. Dr. Wu could recommend a good doctor for Chi's father.

February was cold and I was glad I had bought the warm coat. It was nice to get back to the apartment after a long day at school. Chi still was under the assumption that I was taking sewing lessons at a shop downtown. We were still looking for another apartment, but everything we saw was too expensive. Chi reassured me that something would come up eventually.

I was coming into the store one day when I saw Eric talking to Mrs. Ling. He stopped me as I tried to hurry passed them.

"I guess congratulations are in order," he said. "When is your baby due?"

"June," I answered.

"Are you sure you don't want to do some sewing for my mother? She wants to meet you."

"I don't have much time right now, Eric," I said quietly. "I'm busy getting ready for the baby, maybe sometime later."

I knew later would not come. The money would be nice, but I found it a little insulting that he thought of me as a seamstress who needed money. *After all, my husband had a well-paying job and I was going to be a lawyer*, I smiled to myself. My feelings toward Eric were changing. I still thought he was the most handsome man I had ever seen, but now I was beginning to feel a little leery of him. I no longer felt the way he looked at me was flattering. It frightened me a little bit. He was still nice to me, but I couldn't understand my feelings, both attracted to him and scared of him at the same time.

My financial aid check came in the mail. I cashed it and paid my tuition and I still had over one hundred and fifty dollars left. I took the cash and put it in the box thinking I would surprise Chi when we counted the money next Friday. I will tell Chi that I earned the money sewing for a lady in my sewing class. I didn't need Eric paying me for sewing, I thought to myself. I was still bothered by what he had said and I didn't know why.

School was going well. I was taking English and a math class. The math class was so easy; I had already studied the same problems. The English class was a little more difficult, but still not hard. I joined a small study group in English and we would meet at least once a week. This helped so much and I grew quite fond of the students. They were always full of questions for me about China. I would have to steer them onto the academics.

We usually met on Wednesday mornings at a small coffee shop by the University. I started taking advantage of Wednesdays to shop or sometimes look at apartments after the study group broke up. I explained to Chi that I would look for an apartment every Wednesday. Everything I looked at was too expensive and I actually thought for a moment of taking Eric up on the sewing. But I quickly put that thought aside, I would find another way of making money if I had to.

There was another Chinese girl in our group and one morning she told an interesting story about her grandmother. She said when her mother was young they lived in Chinatown and her grandmother had gone to the store and never returned. She vanished and was never seen or heard from again. She said her grandfather had spent his entire life and fortune looking for her and never found a trace.

I told them about meeting Mr. Wu and how he had talked about the slave trade. I also opened up to them about wanting to be a lawyer and helping to prosecute these evil people. I enjoyed being a part of this group and the feeling of fitting in.

On the next Friday when Chi and I counted the money in the box Chi was surprised at how much was in there. We counted eight hundred and ten dollars, we were almost there. I told him my story of sewing for a nice lady in my sewing class. He didn't mind me taking sewing lessons was happy I had waited to surprise him.

"I think we will probably be able to purchase the cradle soon," Chi said. "The tips at the restaurant have been good these last few weeks."

"That is wonderful, Chi. I could always do some more sewing for Eric's mother," I said rather quietly.

"No, Chan-lei, I don't want you to have anything to do with either of them. I haven't met the O'Malley's but I am a little leery of them.

You have so much to do getting ready for our baby; you don't have to be sewing. I don't mind if you sew for your friends, but not the O'Malley's."

Well, that settled that. I was relieved that Chi felt this way. I still thought about Eric but my thoughts about him had changed. I found him attractive still, but I was also starting to see Chi in a whole new light. He seemed to be bending a bit and not quite as rigid as before. Maybe America was rubbing off on him?

NINE

I LOVED SCHOOL. THE UNIVERSITY WAS ALL I HAD imagined and more. Soon it was March, and I didn't quite know where the time had gone. The baby was defiantly getting bigger and I loved the movement I felt from her. Yes, hey, I still thought girl, but didn't say anything because if the baby was a boy I never wanted anyone to say anything to him about me wanting a girl.

Jenny was now dating a handsome young man by the name of David Cho. She confided in me that this was the first man that she had fallen for. She had never thought of marriage or even a serious relationship with a man before. David was also a student at the University. Soon he was a part of our group. I invited them both over for dinner one night, first asking Jenny to confide in David my secret so he wouldn't say anything about school to Chi.

Surprisingly Chi and David seemed to hit it off right away and Chi was thrilled to have his first American friend outside of the restaurant. David had been born in the United States; his grandparents had emigrated from China many years ago.

The Wu's invited us over about once a month now. Dr. Wu was so kind to me and became more than my doctor and Jenny's mother. I had confided in her about Chi's traditional ways and that I hadn't told him I was going to school.

"I think you should tell him before he finds out some other way," Dr. Wu advised me. "You need to learn to stand up for yourself."

"I'll think about it," I said quietly.

I was fascinated with Mr. Wu and tried to get him to talk about his cases as often as possible. The Wu family also helped me with the constant missing of my family. They were all three so kind and interesting. I still loved the way Jenny flitted around like a little sprite of some kind, she made me smile. But I also missed my parents so much. Why was it taking so long for their visas? Reports were that Chi's father was better, but we wanted them near us. Mr. Wu said he would ask a couple of his friends that dealt with immigration; in the meantime, we would have to be patient.

One evening Mr. Wu started talking about the slave trade. He said the investigators were frustrated because they had a suspect but couldn't find any evidence they could use to prosecute.

"I'm thankful there haven't been any more girls missing," Mr. Wu said. "I think the suspects know we are on to them and are laying low for a while."

"Who do you suspect?" I asked shyly.

"I wish I could tell you, Chan-lei, but it is confidential. I want you to be careful who you make friends with in Chinatown."

"Chi and I are looking for an apartment outside of Chinatown, but we haven't had much luck, everything is so expensive."

"I'll ask around, but did you ever think of finding something bigger that you and your parents could share, and you could share the rent?"

"That is a good idea," I said. "Maybe we could find a house to rent."

When we returned home Chi and I talked about a house big enough for the extended family. One of the nice things about Asian families is that they honor the older family members and have respect for the knowledge they possess and make them apart of their everyday life. I was excited to think about this. Chi was also excited and thought we could look after his father. I would love to have my mother and mother-in-law living with us. One of them would always be there to look after the baby while I attended classes. Maybe that is when I would confess to Chi about school. I wouldn't have to leave her in day care, something I didn't want to do but felt I had no choice. I knew Chi would never let me leave the baby with a stranger.

Soon it was April and our anniversary was coming up. Chi came home one evening with a strange smile. I had no idea what this meant, but I was suddenly excited. He told me he had money to add to the cradle money.

"Chan-lei," he said. "When I was leaving this evening the owner of the restaurant called me into his office. I was scared, thinking I was going to be fired or something. But no, he told me I have been doing a wonderful job and he promoted me to Chef, not Junior Chef but Chef and gave me a raise. He also gave me a bonus of five hundred dollars. Five hundred dollars, Chan-lei, my career is starting to take off."

I was completely shocked, but happy for him. "Oh Chi, I am so proud of you," I said quietly. I wanted to shout it!

"I'm putting it in the cradle box and tomorrow on our first anniversary we will count it and then we will go and buy that beautiful cradle! I'm sure there is more than enough. And then we will go out and have a special anniversary dinner."

I was excited and on the next day, April 12th, Chi took the whole day off work. First, we counted the money in the little black box, over $1,300.00! I dressed in my blue silk dress. It was a beautiful spring day in San Francisco so I only needed a light jacket. We took the cable car to Union Street and went into the little shop to buy our beautiful cradle. It was there, looking more gorgeous than I remembered. The lady in the shop told us a brand new one would be delivered from the warehouse and we should have it within a week, plus she said they were having a sale and we could have the cradle for $800.00. Chi and I were so happy, now we had money left over for other things. We also bought the bedding we had seen before. It seemed like we were walking on air when we left the shop.

We stopped by the apartment to drop off the bedding and then decided to go down to Fisherman's Wharf for dinner. We had never been there before.

"We seem to eat Chinese food all the time," Chi laughed. "I think it's time that we sampled some American food. People at the restaurant tell me that the restaurants on Fisherman's Wharf are delicious and we can do a little shopping at Pier 39. I haven't bought you an Anniversary present yet."

Pier 39 is a tourist place with little shops all along the pier. I had heard it was picturesque but the shops were expensive. I doubted that we could buy anything but it would be fun to look.

"That will be wonderful, but I don't need a present. I have all that I want and I hear it is expensive there."

Chi smiled.

When we arrived at the Wharf we were both amazed at how wonderful it was. We walked for a while and then we spotted a little kiosk that had oysters one could buy, and when opened they contained a pearl. The lady at the kiosk explained the pearls could be anything from a small pearl to a large one. They could be regular pearls or black pearls, but you were guaranteed a pearl.

We selected an oyster, paid the five dollars for it, and waited for her to open it. As she cut the oyster open my excitement grew. I was expecting a tiny pearl, but the oyster revealed a medium sized black pearl.

"Oh look at this Chan-lei," Chi gushed.

I couldn't speak, I was so excited. It was beautiful and looked perfect. The lady at the kiosk had settings the pearl could be set into. Chi thought we should set it into a ring for me.

"In this land it seems ladies wear a ring they call an engagement ring," Chi said. "We can call this your engagement ring."

Why was Chi being so nice? I wondered. I thought of my deceptions, and thought I didn't deserve the ring!

They had settings from inexpensive ones to one with diamonds. After much deliberating we chose a beautiful setting that looked like a clamshell. It only took a couple of minutes to set it, but when I tried it on my finger it was much too large.

"She has such tiny, delicate fingers," the kiosk lady said to Chi. "We can size it for you, but it will take about a half hour to do it."

"That will be fine," Chi said. "We will look in the other shops here until it is ready."

The setting was expensive for us, a little over a hundred dollars, but Chi excused the expense by saying we had saved money on the cradle. Also, they valued the pearl at much more than five dollars, several hundred to be exact. We walked away feeling lucky.

We walked through several shops and bought a couple of baby bibs with local logos on them and soon it was time to check on the ring. It was ready and looked so beautiful when Chi slipped it on my finger. Then Chi thought we should buy another oyster and save the pearl for the baby. It turned out to be a plain little pearl, but we were thrilled. The lady put it in a little fabric envelope. When our baby was old enough, we would have it set in a ring for her or him.

We walked down the Wharf and finally decided on a restaurant that we both thought looked good. They seated us near a window and we could look out on the lights and the water. It was so beautiful, but I kept glancing at my new ring. It looked so pretty I thought. We both ordered lobster and it was delicious. I looked at Chi and he looked so handsome, I felt nothing but love for him. I was falling in love with my own husband. No more thoughts of blue eyes, I secretly thought. And I must stop my deceptions.

As we were leaving the restaurant Chi held the door open for me. As I went out I bumped into Eric O'Malley coming in the door, by himself. At that moment the baby actually lurched inside me, not a kick but a big heave.

"Chan-lei, what are you doing here?" he said.

"Hello Eric," I said timidly, "This is my husband, Chi. We were having dinner."

Chi shook Eric's hand, but he had a strange look on his face. I didn't think he liked him at all.

"So almost time for the baby?" Eric said.

"Not for another couple of months," I said.

Why was he interested in my baby? I had a strange feeling again and wanted to get away from him as soon as possible but Eric seemed to be full of questions.

"You work at the San Tung Restaurant don't you?" he asked Chi.

"Yes," Chi said. "How did you know?"

"Oh, I guess I heard it somewhere, maybe from Chan-lei."

I had never said anything to Eric about where Chi worked. Maybe Mrs. Ling had told him, they seemed to always talk when he was in the store.

"How do you like living in America? It must be so different from China."

"Chan-lei and I like it a lot," Chi said, looking him over. "We came here for more opportunities for our family."

"Yes," Eric replied, "America is full of opportunities."

We finally excused ourselves and started home. I was amazed that Eric knew so much about us. Why?

"So, that was the famous Eric O'Malley," Chi said. "He seems to know a lot about us."

"Chi, I never told him where you work. I have only talked to him a couple of times in the Ling's store and the time he gave me a ride home."

"I don't understand why, but he makes me a little nervous." Chi said. "David talked about the O'Malley's and told me not to trust them. He thinks they have always been involved in some kind of illegal activity. And I did not like the way he looked at you, Chan-lei. I'm a man, I know what that look means, he looks at you like he desires you."

"I don't think so Chi," I stammered. "Look at me, I am pregnant, why would he want me?"

"Some men don't care about things like pregnancy," he said with his eyes downcast.

I was feeling much the same way but didn't say anything to Chi. Maybe I should tell him about the warning note? We hurried home; nothing was going to spoil our wonderful anniversary day so I didn't say anything else. We didn't talk about Eric the rest of the evening, but I had that uneasy feeling. How did he know where Chi worked? And why did it matter to him? Also it was strange that the baby had reacted so peculiar to him, jumping the way she did. I looked at the ring again and then at Chi feeling I was truly a lucky woman. I would put all thoughts of Eric out of my mind. I had much better things to think about and a bright future ahead. But how was I going to tell Chi about my real classes? He will be angry and never trust me again.

The next week a big box arrived at my door. It was the cradle. I wanted to open it immediately, but held off the longing until Chi came home. I spent most of the time waiting, pacing and staring at the box. When he came in we opened the box together and there were parts to the cradle not the cradle as a whole. We had to put it together ourselves. After much work, and thankfully the instructions were also printed in Chinese we had the cradle together. We put it at the end of our bed and put the adorable bedding in it, and the final touch was the beautiful hand knit blanket the Wu's had given us. Then we stood back and admired it.

The only drawback was still living above the Ling's store. Both of us wanted to move as soon as possible. But I thought about everything we had at the moment, the apartment was warm and cozy and furnished. In a new apartment, or house, we would have to buy furniture. Chi had his new position at the restaurant and more money for us but could we afford more expenses? Soon we would be holding our baby in our arms. Life was good. If only I could tell Chi the truth!

Soon it was May and time for final exams. I enjoyed my study group, probably more for the companionship than anything else. I was delighted that I had American friends now. Jenny and David were frequent guests in our home and we loved visiting at the Wu home often. I was happy, but every time I saw a big black car I had the same uneasy feeling. And I felt I was living a lie.

TEN

I WAS NERVOUS TAKING MY FINAL EXAMS, BUT THEY seemed easy. I knew math would be easy, but was not sure about English. As it turned out, it was not as hard as it could have been. Now I would wait for the results and take the summer off of classes to wait for the birth of my baby. No more lies about where I was going for a while.

I did some more sewing and checked through all the baby clothes. With everything I had bought, my mother had sent me, and the items I had knitted and sewn there was more than enough to welcome this little one into the world. I could hardly wait.

I grew heavier and more uncomfortable, but I had not gained any body weight, only baby. My stomach seemed enormous and I couldn't tie my own shoes. Dr. Wu assured me that everything was normal, but I still wished my mother was with me. I missed her so much and when I thought about her, tears would sting my eyes.

Chi was happy with his new position at the restaurant; he did have to work more hours than he did before, but took every opportunity to spoil me and brought simple little gifts home. One day he came home lugging a rocking chair, it was beautiful. He said he knew I would need it to rock the baby. I felt he was happy with the fact that I was home all the time. He also assured me that he was only a quick phone call away while he was at the restaurant and could be home in a couple of minutes if I needed him. Jenny came over often to check on me and Dr. Wu also was a phone call away. Still, I wanted my mother.

My grades came in the mail, an A in both classes, making me happy. Luckily I usually got the mail before Chi came home. My study group invited me to lunch to celebrate. They chose a little restaurant close by the University. Jenny came over to go with me, she didn't want me *out on the streets alone,* as she put it. Chi didn't either, so I just said Jenny was taking me out to lunch before the baby arrived. It seemed like everyone was watching me.

When we walked into the restaurant I was stunned. The table that my friends were at was decorated and presents everywhere. Jenny quickly explained it was a baby shower, an American custom. I had never heard of such a thing.

"Oh my goodness," I stammered.

"Surprise," everyone said in unison.

It turned out to be a wonderful party. They had a beautiful cake for me, decorated in blue and pink. I received so many gifts, beautiful baby clothes and a gorgeous stroller that they had all gone in together to buy. I couldn't believe that my new friends had put this all together for me. Oh, how I loved my American friends.

Jenny helped me bring everything back to the apartment. When we went through the store Mrs. Ling gave us her disapproving stare.

Chi came home in a few minutes and he was also surprised at all my gifts.

I told him they were from Jenny's friends, another lie. Jenny explained the baby shower custom to him. He was happy for me and couldn't seem to stop smiling.

Of course, it was Jenny that had put it all together.

June arrived and still the baby had not. I spent most of my time in the apartment waiting for signs of labor. Dr. Wu had explained what to look for but I had none of the symptoms she talked about.

We had also attended birthing classes at the Chinese Hospital. Chi took the classes seriously and we had practiced my breathing every day. He was going to be a good coach if the time ever arrived, I laughed to myself.

By the middle of June, I was growing anxious. Dr. Wu examined me and said that everything was fine.

"First babies are often late," she explained. "If nothing happens by next week we will do a stress test to make sure the baby is handling this okay, but the baby seems strong and healthy. You need to be patient, the baby will come soon."

It was hard to be patient, but I kept busy doing some more sewing and knitting. One day when I went through the store to buy some groceries Eric was there.

"No baby yet, Chan-lei?" he said.

"Not yet," I said timidly.

I hurried to get away from him and Mrs. Ling, wanting to be by myself and not have staring eyes on me.

The next week I went to see Dr. Wu at the hospital and she did the stress test. They put some kind of a monitor on my stomach and every time I felt the baby move I held up my hand. After, Dr. Wu said the baby was doing fine and to wait, it couldn't be much longer. She explained that sometimes they induced labor, but that it was best to wait another week or so. I felt I couldn't wait much longer.

On July 1st I woke up early feeling strange. My back hurt more than usual and I felt a tightening in my stomach. It didn't hurt badly, it felt like everything tightened up and then relaxed. Was this labor?

I finally woke Chi and told him what I was feeling. He called Dr. Wu and she told him to take me to the hospital and she would come in and check me.

We took a cab to the hospital. When we walked in a nurse came with a wheel chair and took me upstairs to a room. She explained that Dr. Wu had called and would be there shortly. We had already filled out all the admitting forms earlier so we didn't have to wait.

The room was pretty and set up like a bedroom, not a hospital room. There was a rocking chair in the corner and a couple of easy chairs. Wallpaper was on the walls instead of paint and pretty pictures hung on the wall. The nurse explained that this was a birthing room and the baby would be delivered here.

By now the contractions were more than a little tightening, they hurt. The nurse helped me into a hospital gown and into the bed, took my blood pressure and started an IV in my arm.

Dr. Wu arrived and checked me. She said I was about 3 centimeters dilated.

"It will be a little while," she said. "But you are in labor and we will have a baby today. Do you need something for the pain?"

"No," I said. I was determined to give birth naturally without any drugs.

I was excited, but also a little scared. The contractions became stronger and closer together. I wanted my mother.

It wasn't long until Jenny arrived. She had volunteered to be my birth coach along with Chi. She had watched her mother deliver babies before.

Chi was nervous, but acted calm except he kept biting on his lips. With every contraction he talked softly to me and reminded me to breath. Jenny also held my hand and helped to keep me calm.

I felt a strong contraction and something happened. Suddenly I felt warm water all over me. The nurse came in and said that my water had broken. She changed my gown and the sheets on the bed.

"This is a good sign," she said. "You should go fast from now on."

About noon Dr. Wu checked me again and said I was now 7

centimeters dilated.

"It won't be long now," she said.

The contractions continued. There was a point that I didn't think I could do it any longer.

"Chi," I cried out. "I can't do this. It hurts so much and I'm so tired."

Chi put a cold cloth on my head and said in Chinese, "Chan-lei, my darling, this will be over soon and we will have our beautiful child. You are so brave. A little bit longer. I love you more than you can possibly imagine. Now, take a deep breath and let it out slowly like they taught us in the class."

The deep breathing and Chi's words seemed to rally me and I knew that as long it is would take it would be okay because our beautiful child would be born. From that moment on I kept thinking that every painful contraction was one less to endure before our baby was born, but they did hurt. Oh my, they hurt.

Shortly Dr. Wu came in and announced that I was fully dilated now; the nurses started breaking the bed down to make it into a delivery table. They moved quickly and suddenly I felt my legs being put into stirrups on the table. They also put leggings on my legs that felt warm and soothing.

"You are going to push now, Chan-lei," Dr. Wu said kindly. "When you feel the next contraction I want you to push hard, almost like you are having a bowel movement."

I felt a little embarrassed by this, but I would try. I decided that having a baby was giving up all of your privacy, and your dignity.

When the next contraction came I gave it my all and pushed. It was the hardest thing I had ever done in my life. The next few were even worse and finally I cried out that I couldn't do it any longer.

"I'm going to die." I said.

"No you're not," both Chi and Jenny called out at once.

Dr. Wu said, "I understand how tired you are but I promise it will be over soon. You have to keep going for a few more minutes. Take a deep breath before you push, it will give you energy."

I did as I was told and took deep breaths and all of a sudden I felt the baby move down with the last push and then it felt like everything inside me was being pulled out of my body and there was a baby. Dr. Wu pulled the baby up and said proudly, "You were right Chan-lei; it's a girl, and a pretty girl at that."

The baby gave out a little cry and then was quiet.

"Is she okay?" I asked.

"Yes," Dr. Wu said, "She's being a good baby." She laughed.

I looked at Chi and there were tears on his cheeks and Dr. Wu laid the baby up on my chest and I looked into the most incredible face I had ever seen. She opened her little eyes and seemed to look right at me. We had been told in the childbirth classes that babies only see shadows at first, but I felt like she was seeing me, she knew I was her mother. Dr. Wu was busy with me, delivering the placenta, and whatever. I didn't feel anything; I was so busy looking at my daughter.

"So, what is her name?" Dr. Wu said.

I looked at Chi who was still had tears on his face. "Shall we go with the name we picked if it was a girl?"

"I think so," Chi said with a catch in his voice. "Hello little Lein Hua," he said to the baby.

Lein Hua in Chinese means Lotus Flower, and stood for strength. But we had also discussed that she needed an American name. We had thought of calling her Jenny. But I had also heard an American name that had stuck with me. Mia! I had told Chi that that name sounded American but yet had a Chinese ring to it.

"Shall we call her Mia?" I asked Chi

"Oh yes," he answered. "Lein Hua will be her name but we will call her Mia."

Dr. Wu finished with me. The nurse put a warm blanket over me and gave me a glass of water. She told me to try to drink as much as I could. Then she took Mia and put her on a scale. She weighed 6 pounds 4 ounces and was 19 inches long. She put a diaper and little shirt on her and wrapped her in a little blanket and put a knitted cap on her head covering her dark hair. She had lots of black hair.

Then she put Mia on my breast to nurse. She wasn't sure at first and started rooting around, but after a little coaching and help from the nurse, she latched on to my breast and started to nurse.

A couple of hours later they moved me into another room. Dr. Wu came in and told me if everything went well, I could go home tomorrow.

We made phone calls to our family. It took a little while to get an international line and when my mother answered the phone, I broke into sobs. I quickly assured her that everything was okay, little Mia had been born and we were doing fine. We couldn't talk long because of the expense, but it was so good to hear her voice. I also talked to my Dad for a few seconds. Next we called Chi's parents. Chi cried when he talked to them. Again, I realized how much we both missed our families, not just me.

Chi went to check in with the restaurant and tell them about Mia. The nurses told me they could take the baby to the nursery while I got some rest.

"No," I said, "I'll keep her with me." There was no way I would let this little creature ever leave me. I looked at her and knew at that moment there was nothing I wouldn't do for her. I had never known a love as special as what I was feeling for Mia. I unwrapped her and checked her all over, even her little toes. She had everything. She was perfect. She was the most special and beautiful human being I had seen in my life.

A couple of hours later Chi returned with his arms full of flowers and a big stuffed bear. He was so happy and couldn't wait to hold little Mia.

I thought he was so special. How could I have ever thought of and dreamed about another man. As he gazed at Mia my heart melted, his shiny black hair gleamed and his face looked serene as he held her. I found a new strength inside me, and vowed to tell Chi the truth when we returned home. With the birth of Mia, I felt a new birth inside myself, I would do anything to protect this child.

Chi spent the night at the hospital, sleeping in a chair. Although there was a bassinet in the room, I put the bars up on my hospital bed and put pillows next to the bar, putting Mia there, sleeping next to me. I was quite in love with my little daughter

Chi and I didn't sleep much, we couldn't help but stare at our gorgeous daughter most of the night and whisper about how happy we were.

The next morning, Dr. Wu came in and said that we could take Mia home. They took a couple more tests with both me and the baby and then it was time to go. Chi had called a taxi and we loaded in all our things and headed home.

Chi was carrying my suitcase, flowers and a big bag of baby things the hospital had given us and I was carrying the precious Mia when we walked through the store. Mr. Ling came up and gave us his congratulations. Mrs. Ling looked at us with quite different, a look of disgust and said, "Keep that child quiet."

Chi and I looked at each other but decided this was not the time to start an argument. We nodded and walked toward the stairs.

We went upstairs and walked into our home. Chi put the flowers on the kitchen table and my suitcase in the bedroom. I walked into the bedroom and laid my little girl in her beautiful brass cradle and covered her with the gorgeous blanket the Wu's had given us. She looked like a little princess in the cradle. It made me so happy that we had saved our money for this special cradle.

Chi walked into the bedroom and looked down at Mia, and I looked at him like it was the first time I had ever seen him. He was standing there with such love on his face. For the first time I saw him, only him. He was such a handsome man. He was tall for a Chinese man, almost six feet tall. I looked at his face; he had such an incredibly beautiful face. I think I fell in love with him for the first time. Eric was handsome, but Chi was so much more so, plus he was kind, sweet and even more handsome than Eric could ever be. I knew at that moment that I loved him, more than only loving him as a friend, a playmate when we were children, a man I knew I was supposed to marry. My heart did a little flutter. I would tell him all my desires and not fear the consequences.

ELEVEN

THREE DAYS LATER I WOKE UP FEELING MISERABLE. I heard Mia, and when I got up to go to her my entire chest hurt. I have always been thin and small breasted, but suddenly I was enormous, I didn't know what was wrong. I picked Mia up, changed her and sat down in the rocking chair to nurse her. It hurt more than usual when she started to nurse, tears streamed down my face. Chi came out into the living room a few minutes later and when he saw me he became very concerned.

"What is wrong?" he asked.

I started to cry even more. "I don't know, I hurt dreadfully."

"I think we should call Dr. Wu," he said tenderly.

"I don't want to bother her; it is so early in the morning."

"Nonsense," he said. "She won't mind and I'm so worried about you."

We called Dr. Wu and she was so nice and comforting explaining my milk had come in, and I would be swollen for a little while but the more I nursed Mia the faster it would get better and soon it would not hurt to nurse her at all.

I felt better after I hung up the phone but I was still miserable. Chi was off work for the day, so he would be there to help out. After I finished with Mia and put her back to sleep, I started to fix breakfast.

"Sit down darling, and I will fix breakfast," Chi said.

I sat down at the kitchen table and continued to cry.

"I want my mother," I sobbed. "I miss her so much and if she were here she could help me, she always understands."

I was so close to my mother; she always knew the right thing to do.

"Why is it taking so long for their visas?" I cried. "We didn't plan on being apart this long, I don't understand. I want her here with us, I can't do this alone."

I continued to sob and didn't know why I was being so unreasonable. Everything hurt! I loved Mia more than anyone could imagine but I also wanted my mother. I didn't understand that hormones were racing through my body after giving birth making me so emotional.

Chi was gentle and he said, "Chan-lei, we can go back to China if you want. I know America is our dream, but we can go back for a while and come back to America with our parents. I don't want you to be upset and unhappy. We will have only lost one year, and really, we haven't even lost that, I'm sure the restaurant will hire me back when we return."

"No," I said. "I need to be strong and not such a baby. I need to learn patience. I'm sorry for being so unreasonable. We have so much already and I need to concentrate on being a wife and mother. I'm so sorry for falling apart like this, you must think I'm weak and silly."

"I don't think that at all. What I think is you miss your mother and you have been through childbirth, and need to recover. We should seriously start looking for another place to live. It is hard for you living here and Mrs. Ling certainly doesn't help matters. I'm going to give finding another place my full attention, I don't think it will be long until our parents are here. I miss my family also," he said with tears in his eyes.

"I think that is a good plan and when we see Mr. Wu I will ask him if he knows anyone that can help with visas," I said, starting to calm down.

I couldn't believe how compassionate Chi was being. I had to stop being such a child. I know Jenny had asked her father about an immigration lawyer, but I would also ask him myself.

Chi helped me around the house all day and held Mia while I took a shower and dressed. Dr. Wu had said that warm water would help and I let the shower run on my chest for a long time. Amazingly it felt better, and the next time I nursed Mia it still hurt, but not as much. I vowed to be strong and not complain so much.

The next day Jenny came over and stayed most of the day while Chi was at work. She was such wonderful friend and completely enamored with Mia. I teased her that she should hurry and marry David so she could have a baby of her own.

Later she said, "I think you need to start getting out more after you recover from the birth. You have been cooped up in this apartment before and after Mia's birth for a long time."

"I know," I said, "but I'm not sure where to go. We want to look for another place to live, maybe we could go apartment hunting? I don't like living here anymore with Mrs. Ling's attitude."

"There is something very wrong with that woman," she laughed. "She gave me the once over when I came in just now."

"It is very hard to be around her, although Mr. Ling is always very nice. I almost think he is embarrassed by her attitude. Another thing that bothers me is I have caught her laughing with Eric O'Malley on more than one occasion."

"Eric scares me," Jenny said. "I don't think he is up to anything good. He may be good looking and act charming, but I think it is a ruse."

"To tell you the truth Jenny," I said pensively. "I used to think Eric was the most handsome man I had ever met, but now I see him as a little scary too. He seems to show up at the strangest places. Did I tell you he showed up when Chi and I went to Pier 39, when we were leaving the restaurant? I bumped right into him."

"Really?" Jenny looked a little frightened. "Chan-lei you need to stay away from him; I think he is fixated on you and not to be trusted. Maybe he has a crush on you."

"It will be okay," I said. "I'm polite to him but I get away as soon as I can. Now that I'm a mother maybe he will leave me alone."

"I hope so," Jenny said, "but please be careful. I will feel better when you and Chi find another apartment."

"Me too," I said, "me too."

"Have you met his mother?" Jenny asked.

"No, I haven't."

"I have and I don't like her. She is pretty and is always dressed to the nines, but there is something I don't like about her. I think it is her eyes, she has cold eyes."

"What does dressed to the nines mean?" I asked.

Jenny laughed. "She is well dressed, expensive clothes."

We left it at that and Jenny started to tell me about a restaurant called "The Cliff House." She said it sat on a cliff overlooking the ocean.

"They have the best brunches there," she said, "and you can watch seals play on the rocks below while you eat the most delicious food. I think you and Chi should have a double date with David and me. And of course, Mia too."

"What is a brunch?" I asked feeling a little dense.

She explained a brunch to me, and we agreed to go as soon as I was feeling like going out. It sounded like so much fun.

I talked to Jenny about how much I was missing my mother and how I couldn't understand why it was taking so long for their visas.

"Chan-lei, let me talk to my Dad about this," Jenny said showing concern in her voice. "I'm sure he knows an immigration lawyer he can talk to. Maybe it is something simple that can be fixed. I understand how you feel; I don't know what I would do without my parents close." Tears stung my eyes.

"Chi said we can go back to China if I want to, but I think it is best to give it a little more time. I want them here and Chi's parents too. Chi's father is not well and I'm sure your mother could recommend a doctor for him here. I don't think he is getting good medical treatment in China."

Jenny had tears in her eyes also as she said, "We will pray for this to work out soon and I will see what my Dad can do. He knows a lot of people and I know he will want to help. He said he talked to one attorney, but he gets so busy that he may have forgotten about it. It is not his fault; he works very hard."

"You don't have to bother him, Jenny, I know he is a busy man. I'm going to pray that they are here soon. I know they are as eager as we are, maybe more so, they haven't met their granddaughter yet," I said.

"It is not a bother, Chan-lei, my Dad loves helping."

I stayed in most of the following week and was feeling much better by the start of the following week. Soon little Mia was two weeks old, and I was taking her to visit Dr. Wu for our check-ups. Chi was going with me so we decided to have lunch after the doctor's appointment. Dr. Wu said we could go to her home office. I was very surprised when I got dressed that I could fit into the larger jeans I had purchased at the beginning of my pregnancy. I found a loose shirt that didn't look like a maternity top and when I was dressed I decided I didn't look too bad. I dressed Mia in the green silk dress I had made, it was a little big, but she looked beautiful. Chi was so handsome; we were a beautiful family, I thought without modesty. I wrapped Mia in the blanket the Wu's had given us. Even though it was summer there was still a chill in the air.

Jenny answered the door when we arrived at the Wu's house, I thought Jenny was the cutest thing on earth, well, next to Mia that is. She showed us into Dr. Wu's office and soon Dr. Wu came in, first she looked Mia over, listened to her heart and lungs and declared her perfect. Then she asked me a couple of questions and listened to my heart and lungs and said I was also perfect. We talked about how the breast feeding was going. Thank goodness, it was so much better but I confessed to her that I didn't know if I was going to be able to handle it at first. Then she gave me a name and number of a pediatrician for Mia.

After we were finished we asked Jenny if she would like to have lunch with us. She surprised us by saying she had fixed lunch for all of us.

We went into the kitchen. I love this house, it was so open and airy. Our little apartment seemed dark and dingy in comparison.

"I love this kitchen, Jenny," I said. I can't wait for Chi and I to find another apartment. I would love to have a house but we can't afford that until our parents get here."

"I have everyone at the restaurant on the lookout for a place," Chi said.

"Honestly," Jenny said, "I can't believe how adorable you made your apartment but I do understand how you would like to get out of there. How can you stand living around Mrs. Ling?"

I laughed. "I stay away from her as much as possible. If she says another word about Mia, I may slap her."

Both Jenny and Chi laughed. "I might do it myself," Chi said.

We had a very pleasant lunch, Dr. Wu joined us and wanted to hold Mia, and she kept remarking on Mia's beauty.

When we returned to the apartment Chi and I were in good moods and were laughing and talking when I saw Mrs. Ling talking to Eric. *Oh no,* I thought. Eric walked over and congratulated us on the baby and then looked at Mia

"She is a beautiful baby," he said.

I felt uncomfortable with the way he looked at her. Chi and I were polite but hurried up the stairs as soon as possible.

"That guy makes me feel strange," Chi said at the door.

116

"I know," I said, my good mood gone. "I used to think he was nice but there is something about him that I don't trust."

"I know Chan-lei, and I don't like the way he looks at you and now he had that same look with Mia; I don't like it at all."

TWELVE

I FELT UNEASY ABOUT GOING DOWN TO THE STORE, so for the next couple of weeks I stayed close to the apartment yet again. Chi did the grocery shopping for me, I didn't want to run into Eric and I also wanted to stay away from Mrs. Ling.

Things fell into place with the breastfeeding and taking care of Mia. She was growing fast and at the same time I was shrinking. I marveled when I fit into my original jeans. Gee, I was suddenly a size 0 again. I was feeling better about missing my mother, Chi encouraged me to call her once a week, we could afford that, even more if I was feeling sad. We talked a lot and I told her that Mr. Wu was looking into an immigration attorney for us. We also talked about the student unrest in China. I had seen what was happening in Tiananmen Square on television. I wondered if that had anything to do with the delay in their visas, I couldn't imagine it would. It was always good to talk to her, still, we both always cried when it was time to hang up the phone.

I still had not told Chi about my classes, waiting for the right time, I kept telling myself. I talked to my mother about it and she told me that I should not keep secrets from my husband. She was right, she was always right.

Jenny and David came over often. They seemed to enjoy being with us in our little apartment. Chi had looked at several different apartments, but hadn't found one that suited our needs or that we could afford. I enjoyed evenings with Jenny and David, they loved Mia and were so great to talk to. They talked about a place that we should go, The Cliff House, which sat looking over the ocean. It was a San Francisco treasure, they told us. We wanted to see it but I wasn't sure when I would be able to leave the apartment and venture out into the world again, my entire world being Mia.

In the middle of August, we decided it was time to enjoy a brunch at the Cliff House. On Sunday morning I woke up early, fed Mia and dressed for our double date wearing a pair of black pants, that now fit perfectly, and my red lotus blouse. When Chi saw me he whistled.

"What is that?" I exclaimed.

"The guys at the restaurant told me that is how they tell a lady she is beautiful."

"I guess that is a new one for me," I laughed.

Jenny and David were picking us up in David's car. I got out the car seat that I had received at my shower for Mia. I dressed Mia in a warm romper, Jenny had told me it would be cool at the Cliff House. I also put a sweater and cap on her that I had knitted, she looked like a little angel.

Jenny and David arrived, and they looked so stylish. Jenny had on a beautiful sweater set and pants and David always looked nice. Chi came in from the bedroom, and my heart did a flip. He had on black pants, the green silk shirt I had made for him and a black jacket flung over his shoulder, I could not imagine a more handsome man.

We had a little trouble getting Mia's car seat in the car; none of us had ever done it before. Finally, we put Mia in her seat and Chi and I got into the back seat with her. I sat close to Chi and felt somewhat happy, I was still carrying my secret.

On the ride, Jenny and David filled us in on the history of the Cliff House. The original Cliff House was built in1858. It was remodeled in 1877 after it was damaged in a dynamite explosion. In 1894, it was destroyed by fire on Christmas night due to a defective flue. In 1896, it was rebuilt as a seven story Victorian Chateau. In 1906, it survived the great earthquake with little damage only to burn down on the evening of September 7, 1907. It was rebuilt again in 1914 in a neo-classical style that is the structure that stands today with a few improvements.

When we arrived at the Cliff House, it took my breath away. The gorgeous restaurant, sat high on the cliffs. When we walked into the dining room, I was amazed, the entire wall was glass and looked down on the rocks below and out to the ocean. The hostess showed us to a table overlooking this beautiful scene, and we could see sea lions playing on the rocks. I thought I had never seen anything so wonderful and was so happy that we had come to San Francisco. Nothing in the world could be as beautiful as this.

We all decided on the brunch, a buffet, which we had to stand in line to fill our plates. Jenny and David went first and then they watched Mia while Chi and I went to the buffet table. I was thrilled at the food they served, everything from scrambled eggs to waffles to any kind meat you could desire. I had a hard time choosing, and when my plate was full, we returned to the table.

I could not imagine having a better time. Jenny and David were such wonderful company; the food was so good, and Mia slept contently while we ate. I looked down at the rocks below at the sea lions. Jenny said we could go outside later and there were telescopes that we could see through to watch the seals and sea lions below. I was filled with happiness.

I looked over at Chi, and he had never looked so handsome; I silently gave thanks to God for him. It was wonderful how I had felt this new love for him since our Mia had been born. I looked at Mia and gave thanks for her. We had the perfect family; nothing could ever change that.

After we finished eating, we went outside to the deck and looked through the telescopes at the magnificent scenery. We were all feeling so content and I noticed that David took Jenny's hand as we walked out to the deck. I was hoping they would marry soon and be as happy as Chi and I were. The sea lions seemed to look up at us as we looked at them; what a fabulous scene. I vowed to bring Mia here often and as she grew, she would enjoy the sea lions and seals more and more. And this would be the first place I would bring my parents when they arrived. It couldn't be much longer now; it couldn't be. Mr. Wu had his friend looking into their visas.

As we walked back inside the restaurant, I was smiling and holding Mia. I bumped into someone, and when I looked up, I looked into blue eyes. My first thought was to run.

"Eric, what are you doing here?" I stammered.

"Chan-lei, hello, I would like you to meet my Mother, Helen O'Malley."

All of us, Chi, Jenny and David froze.

I looked at an attractive Chinese woman, and as Jenny would say, dressed to the nines. She wore a black pantsuit with a lace blouse underneath. She had black hair with streaks of gray, and her eyes were large for Chinese eyes; but I also was aware of coldness in her eyes.

"Hello," I said with a shake in my voice. "It is strange meeting you here."

"We come here quite often for brunch," Eric said.

I looked at Chi, and he had a look on his face that was not happy at all. He looked at Mrs. O'Malley, and I could tell he didn't like what he saw.

"Oh, look at your beautiful baby," Mrs. O'Malley said.

I didn't want her anywhere near Mia, and I didn't like the way she looked at her.

"She is a gorgeous child, very beautiful," she gushed and I thought I saw a leer on her face.

"We were on our way out," David said.

"Nice to meet you Mrs. O'Malley," I said politely.

"Please, call me Helen," she said with a smirk to her voice, and she took a long look at me. "You are wearing a blouse exactly like one of mine. Wherever did you get it?"

"I made it," I said with confusion. "I made the one you have as well."

"Oh, I guess Eric did say that he had it made for me. Do you sew for others?"

"No," I said emphatically. "I did a favor for Eric; I don't sew for people."

I wanted to make sure she understood that I was not a seamstress and would not be doing any other sewing for her.

Eric walked over and looked me up and down like he always did, right in front of Chi. My face reddened and Chi had a repulsed look on his face.

"Chan-lei," Eric said with a smile on his face. "You look delightful; it doesn't look like you have ever had a baby."

"Well, I have," I said quickly.

Chi said "Chan-lei, we need to get home."

Jenny and I said our goodbyes and hurried out to the car. Chi and David stayed behind to pay the bill.

"Why did they have to come along and spoil our beautiful day?" Jenny said as we reached the car.

I felt like crying. We fastened Mia into her car seat and got in the car, hoping Chi and David would be there quickly.

"Why does he show up wherever I go?" I asked Jenny.

"As you know Chan-lei, that scares me. This is a big city, and he seems to know where you are all the time," Jenny said with real concern in her voice. "Oh, Chan-lei we must find you a new apartment soon and not let anyone know where you are, especially the O'Malleys and the Lings. Something tells me not to trust either one of them."

Chi and David finally walked up. Chi had a sour look on his face and David did not look happy. When they got in the car, they both talked at once.

"How dare that guy look at my wife and baby like that?" Chi said.

"I wanted to punch him," David said. "Jenny, I don't want you anywhere around him or his mother."

"Chan-lei and I were talking about how she and Chi need to find another apartment. And his mother, did you see the look in her eyes? She looks sinister," Jenny said.

"I think she is sinister," Chi said. "Chan-lei, I'm going to find us another place to live as quickly as I can. Those people scare me, and I don't think it is a coincidence that they seem to show up whenever we go out someplace. From now on I don't think you and Mia should go out alone."

"It makes me sick to think I can't go out alone with Mia. Eric has never done anything to me; he has always been polite, but he gives me the creeps, to use an American term," I smiled.

"Look at how much English she has learned in almost a year," Jenny said.

"Chi and I barely speak Chinese anymore, only when I talk to my parents or Chi's," I said with laughter.

We went back to the apartment; I fed Mia and put her down for a nap. Our moods lifted a bit, but Chi still had that scowl on his face. Jenny and I made plans for lunch the next week. She would come and pick me up, and we would go downtown to the little café we enjoyed so much.

"In the meantime, be careful my friend," Jenny said as she gave me a kiss on the cheek.

When we were safe inside the apartment, I decided to tell Chi about my classes. I put Mia down in her cradle and returned to the living room.

"Chi," I said with a strain in my voice, "I have something to tell you."

"What Chan-lei?" He seemed a little short and I could tell he was still thinking about running into Eric.

I took a deep breath and started: "You remember how I used to talk about getting an education and having a career?"

"Yes, but I thought since we got married and now have a family, that those thoughts were behind you," Chi said.

"They are not Chi, and I have deceived you. I didn't take sewing classes; I took two college courses."

"What!" You lied to me?"

"Yes," I said and tears ran down my face. "I'm so sorry, but it means so much to me and now with Mia even more."

"So you want to go off and leave her to obtain your own selfish goals?"

"I will never leave her. And I won't to go back to school until our parents are here to watch over her. I will never leave her with a stranger!"

Now I was angry too. Mia gave me the strength to say what I wanted to say.

"I want this for all of us, Chi, not just me, and how dare you call me selfish. I do all my household chores and take care of you. Look at Dr. Wu, she has it all, a beautiful home and family and a career. Her family does not suffer."

Chi seemed distracted the next couple of days. He said he was thinking about a new place to live, but I felt he was not telling me the entire truth.

Jenny came to pick Mia and me up for our lunch date, I was so thankful to get out of the apartment. I was beginning to feel like a prisoner in my own home. When we walked through the store Mrs. Ling gave me her usual look and she seemed to take a long look at Mia. We hurried; I did not want her around my baby.

We took the cable car downtown. It was so good to be on a cable car again. I loved the look of the city. The café was as charming as ever and the waitress was sweet and so complimentary of Mia.

"Oh Jenny, it is so good to be out and about again," I said with a big smile. "But I have decided to take next semester off school and concentrate on Mia, finding a new apartment and getting my parents here." Jenny surprised me when she said, "I think that is a good idea and when you go back to school, I can help you with Mia. I don't think you need to leave her in a daycare situation."

I was so thankful for Jenny and her friendship. I knew it was more than luck that I met her on one of my first days in this country. She was responsible for finding me a doctor, her mother, and for getting me to enroll in college. I knew God had his hand in it as he does with everything.

"I finally told Chi," I said. "I think he is mad at me, he has been very quiet since I told him."

"He will get over it," she said. "Just stick to your guns."

"What?"

"That means not to change your mind, he will learn to live with it."

We chatted and had a nice lunch. I asked Jenny about David and she confessed that she was head over heels in love with him. She said they were talking about marriage and if there was a wedding, she wanted me to be her matron of honor, but she wanted to take her time and make sure. My head was filled pictures of Jenny as a bride; she will probably look like a little fairy, I smiled to myself.

Soon it was time for us to be on our way home. We did stop in the little baby shop on Union Street and I couldn't resist a darling little outfit for Mia. The saleslady remembered the cradle and thought Mia was the prettiest baby she had ever seen.

We walked to the cable car stop feeling so happy that we were almost dancing when a big black car drove slowly past to dampen our good moods.

THIRTEEN

THE NEXT FEW WEEKS I STAYED CLOSE TO HOME again. I didn't want to run into Eric or Mrs. Ling, and I didn't want to hear any remarks they had about Mia. Chi would take me out now and then, but only to the grocery store. Jenny came over often, but I was feeling like a prisoner. I longed for the time when I could put Mia in her stroller and walk, walk, walk. During this time, I started reading a lot. I had Chi take me to the library, and I checked out books, mostly novels in English. My reading in English was improving, and I could lose myself in the stories. I enjoyed crime novels and started thinking more and more about going to law school. I found a series about a forensic pathologist and I could get completely lost in it,

One afternoon Chi came home early and said he wanted to talk to me.

"Okay." I said feeling a little tense.

"Chan-lei, I've been thinking about what you said."

"About what?" I said confused.

"Going to school, taking college classes," he said.

"Oh," I said now feeling that he was going to chastise me and forbid me to go to school.

"I didn't want you to do it at first, I thought I made enough money and you could just stay home, but I don't think that would make you happy. And you already took classes and nothing around the house seemed to suffer," he laughed. "So I think you should do it."

I jumped up and gave him a big hug. I could hardly believe he had come around to my way of thinking; I was so happy!

August came and went and soon it was September. I felt a little sad about not going to school this semester, but leaving Mia was not what I wanted to do and I had crossed a very big hurdle. I hadn't seen Eric in several days, maybe it would be okay to start going out again, I thought. But then Chi told me he had seen him in the store talking to Mrs. Ling, so I thought better of it.

The phone rang early one morning. Thinking it was Chi calling to check on me, I was surprised when it was my mother. She sounded so excited and started talking fast in Chinese.

"Slow down," I said, "I can't understand you."

"Chan-lei, my darling, we heard from the immigration department. Our visas should be here in a month or less," she exclaimed with delight.

"Oh Mother," I cried back, "I can't believe it, I'm so happy."

We had waited so long and now they would be here in a little over a month. There was so much to do now, after waiting so long, it seemed there wasn't enough time. I called Jenny immediately and asked her to thank her father. I called Chi at the restaurant, something I never did, he said he had a phone call from his parents with the same news.

When Chi came home, we were both so excited and happy that we couldn't stop talking. We decided that we had to find larger quarters right away.

"Chan-lei, we need to find a bigger place before our parents get here,"

"I know," I said. "This apartment is too small for us, much less our parents, and we can't put them in a hotel. Let's call them and tell them we want to find a house big enough for all of us.

We called my parents back and told them we wanted to find a house big enough for all of us but money was a problem. My parents said they were going to send us money so we could rent a house before they arrived.

The next day we started looking for the perfect house. We knew we couldn't afford anything in Pacific Heights, even with our parent's money, but maybe we could find something close. We decided not to tell the Ling's until we were actually moving, I didn't trust Mrs. Ling not to tell Eric, and we didn't want him to know where we were moving. We would find something nice, and it would not be in

Chinatown although it would be easier for our parents to be in Chinatown; but with our help and the Wu's they would be okay. I thought of looking close to the University. That way I could come home to check on Mia between classes. It would be hard to leave her when I returned to school, but now she would have her grandmothers to watch over her.

The following day Chi was off work, so we dressed nicely and headed out to begin our search for a new place. We started at the University and checked everything we saw listed in the newspaper, nothing looked like what we wanted at all. We were about to give up, when we saw a sign on the corner that said "HOUSE FOR RENT." A Victorian house! It looked like it could use some work, but was adorable. We wrote down the telephone number and went to the nearest phone and called. It was the owner of the house, not a rental agency; he said to wait right there, and he would be over in the next few minutes.

The owner walked up to us, and he was Chinese. We had been worried that no one would want to rent to us when they found out that our parents would be living with us. Many people frowned on renting to more than one family, but we felt a Chinese person would understand.

"Hello," he said. "My name is Mr. Cho."

"Very nice to meet you," we both said together.

Mr. Cho seemed warm and we both felt he was happy that we were Chinese.

We explained our circumstances to him, and he didn't seem it was anything but normal. He showed us through the house, it had four bedrooms and two baths, which fit our needs. The house did need a lot of work; it had old wallpaper and the carpets needed replacing, but it was nothing Chi and I couldn't do. There was a small bedroom next to the master bedroom that would make a perfect nursery for Mia. That too needed painting, but I could imagine it painted a soft color and would be perfect.

We talked to Mr. Cho and told him we could do the work for a cut in the rent. He seemed pleased with that. He asked for references, and we didn't want to give the Ling's as a reference, even though they were our landlords now and knew we always paid them on time. We gave him Mr. and Dr. Wu's names. His entire face lit up. "I know Dr. Wu" he said, "she delivered my son, and I'm aware of Mr. Wu. If the Wu's approve of you, that is all I need."

The rent was more than what we were paying now. But with our parents help, we could afford it. We would never be able to afford it on our own.

Mr. Cho showed us out back to a small yard, completely overgrown. In San Francisco, the houses are close together, sometimes even touching. There was a small walkway on one side of the house and nothing on the other. I looked at the overgrown little yard and saw it as it could be, all neat and clean, flowers planted by my mother and mother-in-law. It would be a perfect place for Mia to play.

Chi gave Mr. Cho a check for the deposit and filled out a lease application. We didn't want to think it over, fearing that someone else would take it before we thought about it. Mr. Cho said he would check Chi's employment and with the Wu's and get back to us, but he didn't think there would be a problem.

We left and went to a small café for a cup of tea.

We were so excited we could hardly contain ourselves. We also called Dr. Wu and told her we had used her as a reference. We hadn't thought she would mind, but we were relieved when she said we could use them as references anytime.

Finally, we returned to the apartment, and it was no surprise when Eric was in the store talking to Mrs. Ling. We said polite hellos and hurried up the stairs. I fed Mia and put her in her cradle and then we called Jenny and our parents. Everyone was so happy. The phone rang and it was Mr. Cho, saying he had talked to Mr. Wu, and he had given us a wonderful recommendation, and said if we needed someone to co-sign the lease he would be happy to do so. Mr. Cho said that would not be necessary. He also said that we could come by and do any repairs or painting we wanted to. We decided to move in about a month so we would be all moved when our parents arrived.

Chi and I were overjoyed. We knew we had a lot of planning to do. And we needed to buy furniture. Our apartment was furnished, the only pieces of furniture we owned were Mia's cradle, the rocking chair and the dresser we had bought for her. We were worried about money, but decided we would be okay. We always managed somehow.

The next day Jenny came over, and I couldn't stop talking.

"Oh Jenny, I can't thank you enough for being my friend and introducing me to your mother."

"I'm so happy that I met you Chan-lei, you have been such a good friend. I have friends, but you became my best friend so quick."

"Please thank your parents for giving us such a good recommendation on the house," I said with a tear in my eye.

"My parents love you and Chi, they would do anything for you," Jenny answered.

We played with Mia and Jenny was still so enamored with her. Mia was smiling now, and when Jenny played with her, she was all smiles, I think she liked the pixie ways of Jenny. I silently prayed that Jenny would marry David soon, and they would have a little one of their own. It would be nice for Mia to have a little playmate when she was older.

We decided to go over to the new house the next week and make a list of the things like paint and other items we would need before we could move in. Mr. Cho had given us a key, but the rent wouldn't start until November 1st. That would give us time to do the house repairs and furnish the house before our parents arrived. We estimated they would arrive around the middle of November. We will have the best Christmas this year; I thought. Hopefully nothing would go wrong.

On Monday, Jenny borrowed David's car and picked up Mia and me. We laughed as we put the car seat in; we felt like we were old hands at it now. As we drove over to the new house, I felt a rush of excitement.

"Oh, look, Jenny," I said as we walked in the door. "This is the ugliest wallpaper I have ever seen. It was an ugly flowered wallpaper that had faded and probably hadn't been pretty even when it was new.

Jenny dissolved in laughter. "It is pretty bad," she said. "First thing to put on our list."

We checked the rest of the house, making notes. It seemed our priority would be to tear down all the wallpaper and paint the rooms. We found we needed a new faucet in one of the bathrooms and light bulbs everywhere. We also made notes of the furniture we would need; it would have to be little furniture. A table to eat on, a sofa and chairs for the living room and we could furnish the parents' rooms later.

FOURTEEN

THE NEXT DAY I WENT DOWN TO THE STORE TO PICK up some diapers for Mia. I told myself I needed to be brave and not let Mrs. Ling and Eric intimidate me. I had Mia in her little Ergo strapped on me. I quickly picked up the diapers and hurried to pay for them and go back upstairs when Mrs. Ling confronted me.

"Why do you never go out without Chi or your sassy friend, Jenny, anymore?" she said accusingly.

"I don't know," I said, "it is easier with the baby and all. No reason."

"Eric O'Malley has asked about you. What is going on between the two of you? She said.

"Nothing," I said boldly, "I hardly know him."   Mrs. Ling smirked as she took my money.

I felt uneasy as I went back up to the apartment. I changed Mia, fed her and put her down for a nap and then called Jenny.

"Hey Jenny," I said when she answered, "Do you want to go over to the new house and start taking the wallpaper down? I'm anxious to get started."

"It will have to be after 2 pm," she said. "I have a couple of morning classes, but I have the afternoon free, and David and I made plans to help you on the weekend.

"Jenny, it is okay if you have too much to do. I wanted to get as much done as possible before the weekend. I can go over there myself.

"No, you will not. I'm free after 2 and I don't want you going over there all alone," Jenny said. "I'll borrow David's car and pick you up around 2:30. It will be fun and I can play with my favorite baby girl."

When Chi came home I told him of the plans I made with Jenny. I also told him about the conversation I had with Mrs. Ling.

"Chan-lei, I told you not to go down to the store alone," he said.

"It was only for a minute," I said "I was perfectly safe. I can't always hide up here."

About an hour later the furniture store called to tell us that our credit had been approved. We made an appointment to pick out exactly what we wanted and sign the papers for the payments, I felt we were truly Americans now.

The next afternoon Jenny picked up Mia and me and we went over to the new house. I was happy all the wallpaper stripping material fit in the diaper bag, I didn't want Mrs. Ling asking questions if she spotted it.

When we walked into the house I was still appalled by the ugly wallpaper. Jenny and I started to laugh.

"Wow, this is ugly wallpaper," I said "The sooner we get this done the better."

We dissolved into laughter again. I could hardly wait until all the work was finished, but it would be fun doing it and talking to Jenny.

I had Mia's stroller with us and she fell asleep in it. I was thankful I had remembered to bring it.

We started stripping the wallpaper in the entry way. Before we knew it, it was all down. It came off the wall in large pieces. But the living room was a larger challenge for us, we had to peel off the wallpaper in little pieces with our fingers. Before we finished, it felt like we didn't have any fingernails left.

At 5:00 PM we quit working and Jenny drove us home. Chi was already home when Mia and I got to the apartment.

"Chan-lei, where have you been?" he said.

"Jenny and I went over to the house to get a head start on the wallpaper. I told you where we were going. We stripped all the paper in the entry way and living room."

Chi's face relaxed and he said, "Oh, I forgot. I was worried when you and Mia were not here when I got home. I'm so sorry, now I remember. Yes, the wallpaper is pretty ugly," he said. "It will be so nice when that hideous paper is gone and the walls are freshly painted. Did you and Jenny have fun doing it?"

"Yes, except I don't think we have any fingernails left," I showed him my red, tattered hands.

"Oh poor Baby," he said and put my hand to his lips and kissed them gently. My heart melted and I turned my face up to him. He kissed me softly, and I thought how much I loved him. Our relationship had changed from being friends to truly being in love. Chi was everything to me, my husband, lover, father of my child and my best friend.

On Saturday I packed a basket full of food. I had sandwiches, fruit and tempting treats, very American. I could hardly wait to get to the new house.

Chi and David were amazed at all Jenny and I had accomplished. By the time we left that evening almost all the rooms had a fresh coat of paint except for the bedrooms. We decided to call it a night and come back the next morning to finish up.

I woke up on Sunday with sore muscles, the work was taxing and I was out of shape. As soon as we move into the house I'm going to start yoga, I promised myself.

When the sun went down on Sunday we had all the painting done. The house looked beautiful and as I stood and looked at Mia's room, I started to cry. It looked so sweet, and the mauve-pink paint was perfect. With her green blankets and the brass cradle, it would be such a gorgeous room for my adorable Mia. My life felt almost perfect, then I remembered the note about blue-eyes and my desire to further my education and I realized that nothing is perfect.

The following week Chi and I picked out furniture being very careful with what be bought. We decided on good quality furniture that would last a long time, but did not go for the very expensive. When the salesman added it all up and told us what the payments would be, we were pleased, we could afford it. The furniture would be delivered in a week and then we could start moving in.

It was already October and the leaves were changing on the trees. Soon my mother would be with me and we could plan for a real Christmas. She would be so thrilled by all the decorations in the city. This Christmas would be the best, nothing like the simple Christmas we had always had in China. I could picture a large tree in the living room with presents under it.

The furniture arrived in a week and looked perfect in the house. There were other things we needed, but that would come in time. David and Chi picked up the bed the Wu's had given us. That evening we were invited over to the Wu's for dinner. We had such a good time as usual and I couldn't stop talking about the house.

When we returned to the apartment, the phone was ringing. It was October 16th.

FIFTEEN

CHI ANSWERED THE PHONE AND HIS FACE WENT PALE. He started talking in rapid Chinese and then he listened quietly. I could tell it was something about his father. When he hung up the phone he turned to me with tears in his eyes.

"My father has had a heart attack," he said quietly. "The doctors say he needs heart surgery to survive."

"Oh Chi," I said. "You must go and be there with your mother."

"How can I do that, Chan-lei?" We can't afford tickets for the three of us."

"We have enough money in the house account for you to go," I said. "Mia and I will be fine until you get back, you must be with your parents. We have the Wu's to look after us. You cannot leave your mother alone."

After talking for a while, Chi was convinced that he had to go. We called and made reservations for him early the next morning. Chi called the restaurant, and the owner told him he must go and be with his parents, and not to worry about the restaurant, his job would be waiting when he got home. I promised to call them every couple of days with an update.

Chi didn't want Mia and me to be alone, but I told him I wanted to stay in the apartment that day so I would be near the phone. I had talked to Jenny, and she assured me that her parents would love for me to stay with them. I felt better knowing Chi could call me as soon as he arrived in China, and I could also get updates on his father. I talked to my parents, and they planned to be with Chi's mother during the surgery.

After Chi left, I cleaned up the kitchen, fed and bathed Mia and then I felt panic being alone. What was I going to do without Chi? I would have to be brave and get through this, I told myself. I prayed that Chi's father would do well and Chi would not be gone too long.

The phone rang, and it was Jenny.

"I have classes until 5:00pm and then I'm going to come over and spend the night with you," she said. "I won't take no for an answer; we will have a girl's night."

Tears started to stream down my face. "Oh Jenny, you are the best friend ever," I said.

"I should be there by 5:30," she cried. "Have to run now, but don't fix dinner. I'm bringing dinner and some surprises for Mia."

After I hung up the phone, I sat for a while and cried. I also prayed again for Chi and his father. *Please God, let Chi be safe and let his father get well and our whole family be together soon, real soon.*

After my cry, I decided to make a dessert for tonight and quit feeling sorry for myself. I baked a chocolate cake and did it all from scratch. But when I started making the frosting, I discovered I was out of chocolate. I would have to go down to the store, white frosting would not do.

When Mia woke from her nap, I fed her and put her in the Ergo. It will only take a minute, I told myself.

The store was busy. I found the chocolate and went to stand in line to pay for it. Mia was looking around now, and she stared at the people in the store, becoming aware of her surroundings. I was almost up to the counter when I heard a familiar voice.

"Where have you been hiding yourself these days?" Eric said.

I turned around to see him right behind me.

"Nowhere in particular, I've been busy."

Eric seemed to be staring at Mia, and she looked right back at him and started to cry. It reminded me of the time we had run into Eric while I was pregnant and she jumped in my stomach.

"Oh, don't cry, little baby," he said. I won't hurt you. You are such a pretty little girl."

I held her closer in the Ergo and began to rock back and forth softly.

"She is beautiful, Chan-lei," he said. "Just like her mother."

"Thank you," I said and Mia stopped crying.

Now it was time to pay for my purchase, and I wished Mr. Ling was working the cash register, but it was Mrs. Ling.

"So you are out by yourself for a change," she said.

I mumbled "yes." I didn't want to talk to her or Eric, and was not going to tell them Chi was away.

As I was going toward the stairs I thought I heard Mrs. Ling say something to Eric about a higher price. What were they talking about? I knew they did some kind of business together, but what?

I was uneasy when I returned to the apartment, like I was waiting for something to happen. I put Mia down and finished the cake and then sat in the rocking chair to read, but I couldn't keep my mind on the book. I pictured Chi on the plane, it was a long flight. *Was he tired, was he missing us?*

And I thought about Eric. *How was I so attracted to him when we first arrived here? How did I not realize Chi was the love of my life? How could I have had that dream about Eric?* Suddenly I realized we had been in San Francisco for a year, it was a year ago today we arrived, and so much has happened. The best being Mia, and the Wu's being so kind to us. And I thought about Jenny. *I couldn't ask for a better friend. Her darling little pixie ways, how she seemed to float into a room. It was a miracle I met her the second day we were in America. She had showed me so much. When our parents get here, I will resume my classes,* I told myself. *I don't care if Chi wants me to be a stay at home mother, I believe he is starting to understand. I will become a lawyer and hopefully help Mr. Wu find the missing girls. I have so much to look forward to. Please Lord, let my father-in-law be well and let Chi be back soon.*

I felt so lonely without Chi. *Why did I have this feeling that something bad was about to happen? I had to shake it off, everything will be okay,* I told myself.

Chi will be home soon, and we will move into our house. My parents will be here soon, and Chi's father will get well and they will join us. We have such an amazing future ahead of us. I must cheer up before Jenny gets here. We will have a fun girl's night and Chi will call and tell me everything is okay.

Mia woke up, I fed her again, and made myself a cup of tea. *Tea always makes everything better,* I told myself. I played with Mia and she smiled so sweetly at me. She was beginning to communicate with me, I loved my baby more than I could imagine. She was the light of my life.

After Mia fell back to sleep, I tidied up the apartment, making it nice for Jenny. I set the table for dinner and sat in the rocking chair knitting on a sweater I was making for Mia. Jenny would be here soon and Chi would be calling. Everything would be fine. It was 5 o'clock and Jenny should be here within a half hour.

Suddenly, everything began to shake.

SIXTEEN

THE ROOM SHOOK, AND THINGS STARTED TO FALL. Pictures on the wall fell, dishes flew off the table. The kitchen cabinets opened, and items fell to the floor. I jumped up and grabbed Mia, she was screaming. I held her close and didn't know what to do. I felt I was falling but managed to stay steady on my feet. EARTHQUAKE!

Should I stay here or run outside? I watched, horrified as things fell to the floor and shattered. *What should I do?* I watched in disbelief as my cake shattered on to the floor. All I could think of was I have to protect my baby. There was a loud noise and glass flew all over the floor and the rocking chair I had been sitting there just seconds before. The front window had shattered. My Ergo was lying by the chair. I reached for it and put Mia in it holding her close to me. Finally, what seemed like hours and was only seconds, the shaking stopped. I stood still comforting Mia and then walked to the door and opened it.

Mrs. Ling was screaming at me to get out of the building.

"This whole building could come down if we have a strong aftershock," she yelled.

First, I reached for the phone to call Jenny, but it was dead. I grabbed the diaper bag and started down the stairs. The stairs were broken in places and I was afraid we would fall. When I finally got down to the store, it was a disaster, groceries were all over the floor and broken glass everywhere. Mr. Ling was standing in the mess looking like he was in shock. Mrs. Ling was yelling in Chinese.

"Is the phone working?" I asked.

"Who cares about the phone stupid girl," she screamed back. "Get out of here before we are all buried in the rubble. I don't care where you go, just get out."

I walked out into the street. There was rubble everywhere. People were running or just standing and looking not knowing what to do. I heard one man say this was a big earthquake, and he hoped there would not be fires like the 1906 earthquake. There was dust in the air and people seemed to all be talking. Someone said something about the World Series and the freeways. I needed to find a working phone. And I wanted Chi!

I stood for a moment wondering what to do. I could take a cab to Jenny's or go to the new house. Did I have my keys? It was almost dark but there were no lights on. I didn't see any cabs on the street and I heard someone say the cable cars were not running. *Okay,* I told myself, *I can walk to the Wu's house. It is far, but I can do it. And maybe Jenny will come driving up.* But she didn't. Mia quit crying and I looked at her beautiful face.

"It will be alright, my sweet girl," I said to her. "We will get to Jenny's house and we will be safe."

Even as I said it, I doubted myself. *What will we do?*

Oh Chi, what will I do? I want you here. I said this out loud to no one.

I started to walk down Grant Avenue. Some buildings looked fine, others had broken glass and rubble all around them. I had never felt so alone in my life. I must take care of Mia and find a safe place for her. I continued down the street praying for a cab to come along. Every phone booth I passed, I stopped to see if the phone worked, none of them did. It was getting darker, and Mia would be hungry soon, what would I do? It was October and it gets dark early. How could I find my way in total darkness? Then I noticed there were lights on sporadically. All the power in the city was not off, I would find something. I had to protect Mia! I could check into a motel and wait for the power and phones to come back on. But I trudged on toward the Wu's hoping I could remember what streets to take. I was used to the cable cars and getting off at my destination. I was sure I could ask for directions if I needed them. If I walked up Grant Avenue to Broadway, I could get to Fillmore Street and then I could find the Wu's house. It is a long walk, fifteen to twenty blocks, but I was strong. I could do it.

Mia was very quiet in the Ergo but I was afraid she wouldn't be for long, I would need to feed her soon. And how many diapers did I have in the diaper bag? I hadn't checked before I ran out of the apartment. Mia was getting heavy and everyone I saw on the street looked as frightened as I was. I heard one man telling a woman the freeways collapsed on the south side of the city and there was damage to the Bay Bridge.

I finally reached Broadway and turned left. This part of the city didn't seem as damaged, I could walk faster. As I began to tire, I saw a small café and it was open. A cup of tea should refresh me. I sat in a booth, and a pleasant looking waitress came over. I ordered a cup of tea and some toast. She smiled sweetly and asked if I was okay.

"I'm okay, just getting a bit tired," I replied. "Are your phones working?"

"No," she said, "we are lucky to have lights. Why are you out alone?"

"My apartment was damaged and I had to leave. I'm trying to get to my friend's house and there is no transportation. Would it be okay if I nursed my baby here? I'm very discreet," I smiled at her.

"Of course it's okay. I'll bring your tea in a moment."

I took Mia out of the Ergo and threw her blanket over my shoulder to nurse her. Mia ate well and the waitress brought my tea and toast. Mia fell asleep and was feeling a little refreshed. I wasn't sure how many more blocks I would have to walk.

When she came back to the table, I asked for a favor.

"Could you do me a big favor? I asked.

"Sure. Honey," she said kindly.

"If I leave you a phone number, will you call my friends when your phones come back on? My husband is out of town and I'm trying to get to their house. Tell them I will walk up Broadway to Fillmore."

"Of course I will do that for you."

She loaned me her pen and I wrote the number on a napkin.

"You can stay here as long as you want," she said. "And they can pick you up when you reach them."

"Thank you," I said and a tear rolled down my cheek. "I had better keep going, I must get my baby to safety as soon as I can."

"I understand," she said, "and I will make that call as soon as I possibly can."

"Ask for Jenny," I said, "and if she is not there talk to Dr. or Mr. Wu. Jenny may be out looking for me."

"I will," she said, "and you be safe."

I sat there for a few more minutes, there was an aftershock, but it was not that bad. I put Mia in her Ergo and started back on my journey.

I was feeling somewhat better, but still tired and stressed. I walked several blocks and then sat down on a bus bench for a few minutes. Mia was being such a good baby; she didn't fuss at all. She had to be as tired as I was and confused. I prayed that the Wu's would receive the waitress' call and come looking for me. I felt fortunate to have friends like the Wu's. I prayed for strength to get to their home. I also prayed for Chi.

I had walked probably five more blocks when all the lights were out on the next block. It was very dark, and hard to see but I could see faint lights up ahead so I kept walking toward the light. Also the buildings on this block seemed a lot more damaged than the previous blocks. There was not one person on the street. The heavy lonely feeling came over me again and I started to cry, I wanted Chi and I wanted my mother. If only they were here! If only we had already moved into the new house! If I had my family, I would not be so afraid. A lot of if's, but, I must be brave and take care of Mia. She is my first responsibility. I was afraid there were looters and someone would harm us. My mother always told me to be brave in a bad situation and walk with confidence. I straightened my back, quit crying, and trudged on. Suddenly, I tripped over some rubble, or stepped in a hole, I was not quite sure and started to fall.

I gripped Mia with both hands to protect her. I landed on my knee, pain shot through my leg. It was like nothing I had ever felt before. I came down so hard and couldn't use my hands to protect myself, I had to protect Mia. I tried to sit up, the pain was horrible and finally got myself to a sitting position. I sat there in the dirt looking at Mia, she was crying but didn't seem hurt. I talked softly to her and assured her we were okay. I checked her all over and she didn't seem to have any abrasions. Then I looked at my knee. My jeans were torn and there was a lot of blood. It was hard to see in the dark, but I could tell I had a large gash across my knee. All around me was broken glass, I must have landed on a piece of glass. Somehow I had to stop the bleeding, get myself up and continue walking. I took one of Mia's diapers out of the bag and wrapped it around my knee using the tapes on the diaper to secure it. Now, I have to stand up! The pain filled my entire leg. I felt all over my leg and didn't think it was broken, but maybe my knee cap was. I began talking to myself, *Please Lord, let me be okay and somehow get to the Wu's house*, I prayed. *I should have stayed in the café until the phones came back on. Please help us. The waitress was so kind to us and she said we could stay there. Why was I so stupid to start walking again?* Tears were streaming down my face but I must not scare Mia, so I took control of myself and quit crying and ranting.

As I tried to stand up, someone took hold of me. Finally, there was someone to help. I looked up and all I saw was **blue eyes**. *Oh no, I said to myself.*

Shirley Nolan

SEVENTEEN

"CHAN-LEI, LET ME HELP YOU, WHAT HAPPENED?" Eric said as he reached to take Mia from me.

I held Mia tight so he couldn't take her.

"I'm okay, I fell over something on the sidewalk," I answered.

"My car is right here, let me take you home," he said.

"I can't go home," I answered. "Please take me to Dr. Wu's house. She will take care of us."

"No," he said sternly. "You are going with me, I have you now."

My heart stopped. What did he mean? The Eric I had once thought of a nice was now confirming my worst fears about him.

"NO," I answered firmly. I need stiches, if you won't take me to Dr. Wu's house, take me to a hospital."

Panic gripped every part of me. My face grew hot and I held Mia even tighter.

I looked at him and his blue eyes turned gray.

"No, you are going home with me," he said with menace. My eyes searched the street for someone, anyone to help me, but the street was deserted.

He picked me up with Mia and carried us to his car. I held on to Mia and he put us in the front seat. Then he got into the driver's seat and started the car. Both Mia and I started to cry.

"PLEASE," I need Dr. Wu. She is my doctor and she will take care of my knee and Mia.

"Shut-up Chan-lei, you belong to me now."

How could he talk to me like that? Everything everyone had said about him was accurate. He was not the kind blue-eyed man I had met a year ago and was strangely attracted to, he was mean and I didn't know what was going to happen next. I knew I had to get away from him somehow. I began to shake and was about to plead with him again when he looked at me with eyes of steel and I fell silent as hot tears fell down my face onto Mia's head.

Jenny was on her way to Chan-lei's apartment when the earthquake hit. She didn't feel the earthquake, being in the car, but she watched as traffic lights fell, and buildings began to crumple. She arrived at the Ling store a little after 5:30. She ran inside to see rubble everywhere. She didn't stop, but ran up the stairs to find Chan-lei's apartment a complete mess with the door open. She looked at the broken cake on the floor. After calling for Chan-lei, she ran back down to the store.

"Where are Chan-lei and the baby?" she screamed at Mr. and Mrs. Ling.

Mrs. Ling answered with a sneer. "She was afraid and ran out, the coward. I have no idea where she went. Get out of here, little girl."

Jenny walked outside, and Mr. Ling followed her.

"Chan-lei did not run out afraid," he told her quietly. "My wife ordered her out, I believe she is walking to your house, but I'm not sure."

"Thank you Mr. Ling," Jenny said. "I will find her."

Jenny got in the car and drove slowly up the street looking for signs of Chan-lei. There was a lot of rubble in most places but then there would be places where everything looked like it hadn't been touched. She drove slowly up Grant Avenue thinking Chan-lei would have walked up Grant to Broadway. But she did not see her anywhere. Then she drove to the new house, hoping Chan-lei had gone there, but the house stood dark and empty. At least it looks like there isn't any damage to it, she thought.

Finally, she went home to talk to her father, praying that Chan-lei would be there. But no, she hadn't made it there.

"Oh Dad, I can't find Chan-lei anywhere. I drove the streets that I think she would take and nothing," Jenny cried.

"She was on her way here,' Mr. Wu said. "A waitress called from a coffee shop on Broadway, Chan-lei and Mia were there. She asked the waitress to call us when the phones came back on. She said Chan-lei told her she was walking down Broadway to Fillmore to our house."

"I drove down those streets and didn't see her. I even went by their new house. I'm going back out, maybe I missed her somewhere," Jenny said.

"I'm going with you, Jenny," Mr. Wu said. "I'm afraid something happened to them."

I begged Eric to take me to a hospital. Tears were streaming down my face again. He looked over at me with a sneer.

"I told you to shut-up. Tears ae not going to make me feel sorry for you, my mother will take care of your knee, and it had better not leave a scar."

"What do you care if I have a scar?" I shot back at him.

"You will find out soon enough, I don't want anything to lower your price," he said.

What was he talking about? What price? I had no idea what he was talking about and then all at once it hit me. All the warning about him, Jenny, the Wu's, and even Chi, not to mention the note. Was I being kidnapped? What about my baby?

If I was alone in the car and didn't have Mia with me, I would open the car door and jump out. I wouldn't matter if it killed me, but I had to find a way to save Mia. We drove into a driveway and straight into a garage and the garage door closed behind us.

Eric came around to my side of the car and roughly pulled me out, pushed me through a door into the house and called out:

"Mother, come here. I have someone for you to take care of."

Mrs. O'Malley appeared looking as harsh as I remembered her.

"Oh, Eric darling, you finally have her," she cooed.

"Yes, but her knee is hurt. You need to fix it and I don't want any scars."

"Let me out of here," I screamed. "I need to get to Dr. Wu, you have no right to hold me here."

"It may be awhile before you see Dr. Wu again, if ever," Mrs. O'Malley said, "you are going to stay with us for a little while."

They both seemed to drag us up some stairs and into a bedroom. By this time Mia was also crying again.

"Shut the brat up," Eric said.

"She is frightened, and she is not a brat," I said.

Then he shoved me on the bed and they both went out and locked the door from the outside. I took Mia out of the carrier and held her close, kissing her little head. She needed a diaper change and somehow I must comfort her and not let her be as panicked as I was. I crept over to the door and tried it, locked! I looked around the room, it was clean but very stark, no pictures on the tan walls, just a bed and dresser. There was another door, opening it, it revealed an equally stark bathroom.

Eric must have picked up the diaper bag because it was lying on the bed. I changed Mia and began to hobble around, rocking her in my arms. She cried herself to sleep exhausted and scared. Then I noticed a window. I tried to open it but it was also locked. I noticed there was a trellis with flowers growing on the side of the window. *If I can break the window and somehow get to the trellis, maybe I could climb down before they discovered me. But how was that possible with my hurt knee and Mia? I will find a way,* I told myself.

I began to panic again, my heart felt like it was pounding out of my chest and I felt hot and cold at the same time. Thoughts were racing through my head.

This is all my fault, I'm so selfish. I was the one that wanted to come to America, I had convinced Chi. I had the big desire to become a lawyer and save the world when all Chi wanted was for me to be a wife and mother. If we had stayed in China we would be with our family. So what if Mia was the only child I could have? At least she would be safe now. Would it have been so bad to just be a wife and mother? I thought of my mother and how much she must miss me. *I should have stayed in China, I should have been happy to have one child and a grandchild for my parents. What am I going to do now?*

Jenny and Mr. Wu searched the streets for hours. Finally, they went back to the house hoping against hope they would find Chan-lei there.

"We need to put our heads together and figure out where she could have gone," Mr. Wu said.

"She would come here where she feels safe," Jenny said, "Dad what if we are right about Eric and he has taken her? Let's go to his house and find out."

"I can't go marching in there without a search warrant, Jenny. And I would need evidence to get that. No Judge in his right mind would sign a warrant with my suspicions."

"I know you are right, Dad, but we can get evidence. I have a strong feeling something bad has happened to her and the baby and I think it is Eric O'Malley. Very strange that he seems to show up any place Chan-lei goes. He showed up on Pier 39 on their anniversary. Also at the Cliff House when David and I were with them. Chan-lei has told me she sees his car following her, she thought she was crazy but I don't think so, I think he has been plotting this for a long time."

"I'm worried about him too. I've been trying to link him to the missing girls, but haven't been able to find any concrete evidence as yet. As soon as your mother gets home, let's drive by the O'Malley house and see what we can see. I know where it is."

At that moment the phone rang, and there was another large aftershock. Mr. Wu answered and it was Chi.

"Mr. Wu, this is Chi Wah," he said formally. "I heard about the earthquake and have been trying to call Chan-lei and can't get through to her, are they okay?"

"Chan-lei and the baby were in your apartment when the quake happened and she left. We think she is okay, trying to get to our house. I understand from what Mr. Ling told Jenny, that Mrs. Ling was very mean to her and made her leave. Jenny and I are looking for her. There is a lot of damage to the city and we could have missed her."

"That Mrs. Ling is a very mean lady," Chi said. "You have to find her. Maybe she went to our new house?"

"Jenny already checked there," Mr. Wu said trying to reassure Chi.

Mr. Wu asked about Chi's father and he said he was still in surgery and they would know more in an hour or so. As soon as Chi knew about his father he was taking the first plane back to San Francisco.

"We will take care of them as soon as we locate them," Mr. Wu said.

He wrote down Chi's phone number in China and the hospital and promised to call as soon as he found Chan-lei.

"All I can tell you now is Chan-lei and Mia are missing."

EIGHTEEN

"DAD, I'M SO WORRIED," JENNY SAID, "WE MUST FIND Chan-lei and Mia soon."

"Honey, I'm worried too," Mr. Wu answered, "and sorry to tell you this, if she has been kidnapped for the slave trade it might already be too late, they ship these girls out quickly. That is why it is so hard to catch them."

"What about Mia?" Jenny asked, "will they take her with Chan-lei?"

"No, they will put her in a home until she is old enough to be a prostitute herself or sell her to a family wanting an Asian baby."

"We can't let that happen," Jenny cried. "We have to watch the O'Malley house in case she is there."

"I'm going to do what I can, but without direct evidence, I can't use county money for surveillance, but let me see what can be done."

Mr. Wu went upstairs to change his clothes and Jenny called David to tell him what was happening.

"We need to watch the O'Malley house day and night, David", Jenny told him."

"I can help you do that," David said with compassion. We have to save Chan-lei and Mia; I owe that to Chi for being such a good friend."

I paced the room, mostly hobbling on my hurt leg, when Mrs. O'Malley came back. She was carrying some antiseptic and bandages.

"Take off your jeans and let me look at your knee," she ordered.

"No," I said, "I will not."

She took a hold of my pant leg and roughly tore the whole leg off my jeans.

"There," she said, "there is more than one way to do this."

She ripped my diaper bandage off. I looked at a large cut and the rest of my knee looked like ground meat. The cut was still seeping blood and I could see pieces of glass in it. She poured the antiseptic on the cut and pain gripped me.

"There," she said, "that should do it." putting some gauze on the cut and taping it to my knee.

"Mrs. O'Malley, please," I said, "this is a serious cut, I need a doctor to clean it out and sew it up. Please, I beg you, take me to Dr. Wu or a hospital."

She didn't answer me, she got up and walked out, locking the door behind her. She returned in a few minutes with something white.

"Take off those filthy clothes and put this on," she ordered.

It was a very sheer nightgown.

"I can't wear that," I said, "don't you have a robe or something?"

"No, you do what I tell you to do," she fired back.

"I will not," I said with venom.

With that she raised her hand and slapped me across the face. It sounded like a shot and my hand went up to my face. It woke Mia and she started to cry.

"From now on you will do what I tell you or you will get worse next time. Now put that nightgown on and shut the brat up," she yelled.

She left, slamming the door and locking it. I picked Mia up and comforted her, carrying her into the bathroom and looking at my face in the mirror. A large red welt was forming on my cheek. I took Mia back to the bed, nursed her until she calmed down and fell asleep. Panic gripped me again. *What was I going to do?*

In a little while, I took off my dirty clothes and slipped the clean gown over my head. I left my bra and panties on but it was still too sheer so I took the blanket off the bed and wrapped it around me and knelt beside the bed to pray:

Please Lord, let me find a way to get out of here. Please keep my baby safe. Let someone find us, please. If you can't save me, please save my baby. She does not deserve this. Also please take care of Chi and the Wu's. Let them know how much I love them and my parents. I'm sorry for anything I did to bring this about. Please forgive me."

I fell asleep fitfully with Mia in my arms. I would not let go of her, afraid they would take her from me.

Dr. Wu came home. She had been taking care of people hurt in the earthquake. Jenny and Mr. Wu brought her up to date on Chan-lei and Mia.

"We must find her as quickly as possible, she might be hurt," Dr. Wu said.

"Oh, Mom," Jenny cried, "I'm afraid Eric O'Malley found them. I'm so scared."

"Let's go there and find out," Dr. Wu said.

"I think you should stay here Dear, in case she does find her way here," Mr. Wu said. "Jenny and I will go look around the O'Malley house and see if we can find something. I can't go in there without a warrant, but I intend to ask some questions."

I woke up after only a few minutes, everything was very quiet. I felt disoriented and wasn't sure what time it was. *Oh Lord, what am I going to do? I have to get out of here.* I looked at Mia, and started to make a plan. First, I would appeal to Eric. He had acted as my friend before, maybe I could reason with him. If that didn't work, and it probably wouldn't, I would have to find another way. If I could find something to break the window with. I looked in the diaper bag, nothing heavy enough in there. I looked in the bathroom, nothing!

I felt so filthy, I wanted to take a shower but I couldn't leave Mia alone. I wrapped her in the bedspread and laid her on the bathroom floor. I must watch her every minute so they couldn't sneak in and take her. It never dawned on me that if they wanted to, they could take her from me easily. I got out of the shower as quick as possible and put my dirty underwear back on and the nightgown. I changed Mia into a clean outfit I found in the diaper bag and then washed out her other outfit with bath soap. It amazed me how dirty we had become in such a short time.

I loosened the bandage on my knee and looked at how bad the wound was. Panic gripped me again! The Wu's would be looking for me; they wouldn't give up. And Chi, when he found out, he would never stop searching for us.

Jenny and Mr. Wu drove up to the O'Malley house. Lights were on but when they rang the doorbell, no one came to the door.

"Someone is in there," Jenny said. "Maybe we should keep ringing the bell."

"No," he said, "they are not going to answer, but I will come back in the morning and check again. In the meantime, I think someone should watch the house so they don't take her away without us knowing. My instincts tell me Chan-lei is in this house."

"She is here alright," Jenny answered. "David said he would help, maybe he and I could take turns tonight."

"That is a fine young man you have met," but I don't think you should be out here alone. I will take turns with David tonight, you need to get some sleep; you will need it for tomorrow.

I heard the doorbell ring and was surprised when I didn't hear the door open. Maybe it was Jenny? I knew they wouldn't let her in.

Later, Mrs. O'Malley came back with a tray of food.

"Eat this, you will need your strength for your voyage," she said.

"Please, may I talk to Eric?" I said nicely.

"He is busy making arraignments, besides there is no way you can talk him out of this. I'm sure you have that in mind," she said with a frown. She left and I heard the familiar click of the lock.

The food was Chinese and it tasted okay, not like what Chi made, but is wasn't terrible. I took a few bites, I had to eat to keep my strength up to nurse Mia. Also she had brought a cup of tea that made me feel better. Now, I must plan what to do.

I walked over to the window. If I couldn't find a way to break it, maybe I could leave a message on it. But when I looked out, it was to a backyard. no one would see it. Somehow I had to get out that window.

I started to develop a plan. I could use my hand to break the window. Maybe if I wrapped a towel around my hand, I could break it with my fist. But, I must be quiet, they couldn't hear me. I would wait and try to reason with Eric. If that didn't work, I would break the window even if it cut me. I was already hurt, what did another cut matter?

It seemed like hours and finally Eric came in.

"My mother said you wanted to see me," he said looking down and not at me.

A good sign, I thought.

"Eric," I stammered, "I thought we were friends. Why are you doing this to me?"

"I tried to be more than friends with you, Chan-lei, "I wanted to have a love affair with you, but you rebuked me at every turn," he said still looking down.

"I'm married, Eric, and I love my husband."

"You love that weak, shallow man?" he raised his voice. "He is not half the man I am. He is a cook, I'm rich and could give you riches." I chose my next words carefully.

"First of all, Chi is not a weak man, and he is an excellent chef, not a cook. We have loved each other since we were children. I will admit I was attracted to you when we first met," I flattered him. "But I do love Chi and we have a baby. Please understand, we are a family. Please don't do this to me. Let us go and I promise I will not tell anyone. I will go to the Wu's house and simply tell them I got hurt and lost."

"I can't let you go; you know too much. That horrible Wu man has been after me for a long time. Why did you have to make friends with that family?"

"I won't tell, I promise. No one will ever know."

"You could send me to prison, I can't take the chance," he said sadly.

Then he took my face in his hands and kissed me. It was a soft kiss, not rough and mean. He let me go and left the room. Maybe his feelings for me would work after all.

NINETEEN

A FEW MINUTES LATER, ERIC RETURNED. 'CHAN-LEI, THERE is no way I can let you go, if only you had loved me, this wouldn't have happened. But now I don't care who has you," he said.

I decided to take a big chance, I had nothing to lose. Maybe he did care for me still and if he thought I cared he would let me go. I would have to do things I didn't want to do, but I would do anything to save my baby. I didn't find Eric attractive at all anymore, but I could pretend. I could do this, for Mia. I leaned closer to him.

"Eric, I do have feelings for you. I have always thought you the most handsome man ever. I do love Chi, but he is not like you. We would have to be discreet, but we could be lovers, Chi will never know."

Suddenly, he pushed me away and yelled:

"LIAR, you would say anything to get out of this. I don't believe you for a second, you would turn me in and laugh about it."

"I won't, Eric," I pleaded, "Please Eric, please!"

"I can't take that chance. You are like all women, conniving and evil," he still shouted.

"I have never been conniving and you know I'm not evil. I love my family and only want what is best for them. Boy, your mother did some job raising you," regretting my words as I said them.

I thought how evil Helen O'Malley was to me. I knew at that point I had lost my chance at being seductive. I was not good at this at all.

"You leave my mother out of this," he shot back. "She only did what was best for me."

"I know your father died when you were young, how old were you?" I said pretending to care.

"I was six," he surprisingly answered back. "Someone broke into our house, and he was shot."

"How awful but then your mother raised you to sell young girls?" I decided I had nothing to lose at this point.

"She only did what she had to do to support us. She wanted to raise me in wealth, not poverty," he said.

"What did your father do for a living?"

"He was a goody-goody lawyer like your friend, Wu," he said. I could sense a sadness in his voice.

"I wish you were more like your father and not your mother," I said.

"Don't talk about my mother, she is the reason I have what I have."

At this point he stood up to leave. He was white as a ghost.

"Eric, can you do me one favor?"

"What now? No, I can't let you go," he said with exasperation.

"I need diapers for Mia. Please, can you bring me some? Oh, and a pair of tweezers, there is glass in my knee and I can't get it out with my fingers."

"My mother said she took care of that," he said.

"She only put antiseptic on it."

I took off the bandage and showed him my knee. It was red and swollen.

"Please," I begged.

As he looked at my knee, his eyes grew big and he seemed to look sick. He went toward the door.

I sat there looking at the door for a few minutes. I had lost my chance; I was very bad at being a seductress. What was I going to do now?

David arrived at the Wu house later than evening. He talked with

Jenny and Mr. Wu about their plans and then David and Mr. Wu left for the O'Malley house. They took both their cars so one of them could leave for a while and they wouldn't let the house go unwatched.

They both parked across the street in the dark and David got into Mr. Wu's car. In about an hour's time Eric left in his car. David decided to follow Eric while Mr. Wu watched the house.

"Be very careful, David," Mr. Wu said, "I don't trust him at all, he could be carrying a gun."

Eric drove to a grocery store and David went in pretending he was shopping. He wasn't sure if Eric saw him, after all they had only met once, maybe Eric did not remember him. David watched Eric buy some groceries and baby diapers.

David did not follow him back to the house; he took another route so Eric would not be suspicious. When he returned, Eric's car was in the driveway. He hurried to Mr. Wu's car.

"Very interesting," David said to Mr. Wu. "He bought baby diapers."

"I know she is in this house, Mr. Wu said. "We cannot leave this house unwatched for a minute."

David got back in his car and drove to a phone booth to call Jenny.

"She is in the house," he said as soon as Jenny answered. "I followed Eric to a grocery store and he bought diapers. There is no other reason he would buy diapers."

"Poor Chan-lei," Jenny said sadly, "we have to get her out of there."

"We will, we will," David said.

"David, please be careful."

"I will do that," he said.

Chi called a little later and Jenny filled him in on what was happening. Jenny and her father both agreed they couldn't keep anything from Chi. He had a right to know what was happening. She asked about his father.

"The surgery is over," he said. "The doctor told us it went well. As soon as I see him, I'm heading to the airport. I'll get the first flight back; I have to find my family. Chan-lei's parents are here; they are so worried. I didn't tell them everything, just that she is missing in the earthquake. We have to find her," he said with desperation.

Mr. Wu and David sat together in the car.

"Mr. Wu," David began.

"Please," Mr. Wu interrupted, "call me Charles. I have a feeling we are going to be family.

David blushed and then said:

"Do you know how Mr. O'Malley died?"

"Yes, it is a cold case in the DA's office. It happened over twenty years ago, he surprised an intruder in his house and was shot."

'Wow, do you know much about him?"

"Not a lot, David. He was an attorney. His name was Patrick O'Malley, an Irishman. He was a good lawyer, practiced family law and made a very good living."

"Was he involved in the slave-trade or any other shady things?"

"No, I think he was a good man, a straight shooter, as they say."

David and Charles sat in the car looking at the house in silence. Charles was thinking hard.

"Okay, David, I'm going to tell you everything I know about Patrick O'Malley but you have to promise you won't tell anyone, not even Jenny."

"I promise," David said sincerely.

"Alright David, I believe you. Patrick O'Malley was an extremely good attorney. He was ethical and admired by the entire legal community. Even in a large city, the legal community is very small, everyone seems to know everything about each other. He met

Helen Lee in a nightclub in Chinatown, she was a bartender and extremely beautiful. I believe he fell in love at first sight with her and soon they began a love affair. I also believe Helen was only after one thing, and that was money. Patrick made a nice living, but he was not a wealthy man, he spent a great deal of money on Helen buying her jewels, flowers, clothes, even a car and always took her to the best restaurants.

"It wasn't long before Helen became pregnant. Patrick was thrilled and wanted to marry her immediately. Helen was not so sure; she was using Patrick until a richer man came along. But she had no one else to pin the pregnancy on so they married and moved into a nice house in Pacific Heights."

"Things went well for a time and Helen gave birth to a son, Eric Patrick O'Malley. He was a beautiful baby, Chinese, with bright blue Irish eyes. A perfect combination of Helen and Patrick. "

"Life was good after Eric was born. Patrick doted on his son, but soon Helen grew bored, wanted a divorce, she still held on to plans to marry a millionaire, but she knew Patrick would never give up his son. She cheered herself up with alcohol and spending money. She probably had affairs with other men, but I'm sure they quickly caught on to her schemes for riches. Poor Patrick worked hard to make money so his wife could spend it. Time went by and when Eric was about six Patrick surprised an intruder in their home and he was shot and killed. Both Helen and Eric were supposedly asleep upstairs."

"Helen was suspected of hiring a hit-man but there was no proof so she cashed in the two-million-dollar life insurance and lived high off the hog for a time. She bought the million-dollar home they live in now. The intruder was never caught."

David listened intently not saying a word. Finally, he said:

"Is the case still open?"

"It is a cold case, but murder cases are always open. There is no statute of limitations on murder. I still believe she had something to do with it. I wasn't a prosecutor back then, it was over twenty years ago, but I have reviewed the case many times. Have you ever met Helen O'Malley?

"Once," David answered, when Jenny and I went to the Cliff House with Chi and Chan-lei. Eric showed up when we were leaving and his mother was with him."

"What did you think of her?"

"She was cold. She has dead eyes, like a shark."

Charles smiled. "I know," he said.

After Eric left, I sat on the edge of the bed for what seemed hours thinking of what to do. I had to get out of that house somehow. Mia had fallen asleep again. I looked at her beautiful face.

"Oh Mia, I love you more than anything in this world. I will find a way for us to get to safety," I said to my sleeping baby.

The door opened and Eric came in carrying a grocery bag.

"Here are your diapers," he said gruffly.

"Did you bring the tweezers?" I asked.

"They are in the bag," he said.

He started to leave, but turned around and looked at me.

"Chan-lei, tomorrow men are coming to look at you. They will decide your price."

"Men? Price? What are you talking about?" I tried not to sound to panicky but it was hard to hide.

"You do know you are being sold? In the next couple of days, you will board a ship for Burma. You will enter a brothel and learn to pleasure wealthy business men."

I grabbed Mia and shouted:

"A brothel, what are you talking about? What about my baby?

"If you cooperate with me, the baby can stay with you until you reach Burma. But if you fight me, she will be taken away now. In Burma she will be put in a home and raised to follow you into the brothels when she reaches fourteen or fifteen. If you work hard and don't give anyone any trouble, you can see her once a month. If not, you will never see her again."

My blood ran cold.

TWENTY

"WHAT ARE YOU TALKING ABOUT? BURMA? Why are you doing this to me? You know they will find me and you will be in very big trouble. Let me go, no one will ever know. Eric, I promise, no one will know," I cried out.

"I can't let you go, if not for myself but for my mother. She has raised me alone since my father died, I will never let her down." Eric said looking a little sad.

"When did your father die? Tell me what happened," I thought if I could keep him talking, he would change his mind about keeping me."

"I told you, I was very small, but I remember him well. He used to take me with him a lot, even to work. We were in our house late at night. He heard a noise and went downstairs to investigate. A man was in the living room stealing all our belongings. Dad confronted him and the burglar fired a shot, it went right through Dad's heart.

When my mother heard the shot, she ran downstairs, but it was too late."

"What happened after that," I said pressing for more.

"Dad had a large life insurance policy. Mother bought this house and we lived well for a few years. About the time I was in high school, money was dwindling so Mother had to find some way to support us."

"She couldn't get a legitimate job?" I said sarcastically.

"You don't understand; my mother is a lady who has always been pampered. A mundane job was out of the question."

"So she stole children and sold them into slavery? Really nice mother you have, Eric!"

"I told you, don't talk about my mother that way, she did what she had to do," Eric said trying to justify her actions.

But I didn't think he believed it himself.

"Eric, you don't have to be like her, people like you, you have a charm few people possess. Walk away, you don't need her, you are smart and good looking, you could do anything you want. Did you go to college?" I asked trying to play on his emotions.

"No, I didn't have time for that!" he said and his expression changed. His blue eyes turned to steel gray again.

"It's not too late Eric, you could go to college now, I can help you."

He got up and left, slamming the door behind him.

I heard the lock click.

The door woke Mia so I changed and fed her. When she was settled, I examined the window. There had to be a way to break it, but how was I going to get down the trellis with Mia?

I sat down and took the bandage off my leg. It looked horrible, the red places had turned to black and blue and it had swollen even more and was hot to the touch. I pulled out another piece of glass with the tweezers. I didn't see any more glass but I knew there had to be more. I needed a doctor.

It had been quiet for hours as Charles and David sat in the car surveilling the house. Charles decided he had to do something, they couldn't sit there doing nothing.

"David, will you be okay for another couple of hours if I go home and make a couple of phone calls? Charles asked.

"Of course, I can sit here all day, but I do need to make a couple of calls myself and explain where I will be today."

"I also need call my office and tell them I won't be in, and talk to my lead investigator on the missing girls and fill him in on Chan-lei. Maybe he can find a judge that will issue a warrant. She has to be in that house. David, run over to a phone and make your calls and then I will go."

Mr. Wu drove home, he was tired but there would be no sleeping until he had Chan-lei and Mia out of that house. Jenny met him at the door, she hadn't slept either.

"Tell me, what happened during the night? "she said excited.

"Eric went to the store, David followed him and watched as he bought diapers. She has to be there, why else would he by diapers? Where is your mother?"

"Mom went to take care of a pregnant woman who was hurt in the quake. She might be in premature labor so I'm not sure how long she will be."

"I need to make some calls and then go back and relieve David, he has to be exhausted. I have to say Jenny, I really like that young man."

"I'll go back with you Dad," Jenny said. "I'm sure Chan-lei is not going to show up here, I think we both know where she is."

Mr. Wu called his office and Jim Travis, his lead investigator had just walked in.

"Jim, I need your help. I am pretty sure we have another missing girl and I'm also sure I know where she is being held. I'm going to fax you a motion for a warrant. Please get it signed if you have to go to every judge in San Francisco and then meet me at the

O'Malley house, also bring the SWAT team."

I fell asleep with Mia in my arms but did not sleep long. Mia woke me up hungry and in need of a diaper change. I looked over at the window and felt scared, men were coming to look at me? I was a prisoner in this house? Did I have enough diapers for Mia? What was going to happen to us? I had to do something about the window but I must be careful because I was not sure when Eric or his evil mother would come in. It was very early in the morning, hopefully they were sleeping.

I went in the bathroom and found a towel. My knee was hurting and every step was painful. I had a headache, and felt warm, but I couldn't worry about this now. Wrapping the towel around my hand I hit it on the window several times, nothing happened.

Finally, I gave it a good hit feeling frustrated. I felt it give, and the door opened.

Eric walked in with three men, two Asian and a Caucasian, and they looked mean. I pretended I was drying my hands on the towel, but I quickly went to the bed and picked up Mia and the blanket to wrap around me.

"Put the child down and come over here," one of them said.

I was defensive and I shouted, "Don't touch her or me!" I shouted.

"Or you will do what, stupid girl? You will do as you are told!" the

Caucasian man said.

I looked at Eric, he walked to the door and left me alone with these men. *Could he not look at what they might do?* I thought. One of the Asian men came over to me, he looked me up and down, then tore the blanket off me and lifted up the nightgown. Immediately I reacted and ran from him. He reached out and grabbed my arm.

"Let me look at you," he said.

He grabbed Mia and threw her on the bed, she started to cry.

"You leave me alone," I screamed, "and don't you dare touch my child. When I get out of here you will go to prison," not sure where this bravery came from.

I started toward the bed to console Mia but the Caucasian man raised his hand and hit me so hard, I seemed to fly across the room and hit the wall with a force I could not comprehend. Pain filled my head and went through my body. I had never felt anything like this before, everything turned black for a moment and I fell to the floor. I could feel pain in my knee and blood running down my leg.

The man picked me up roughly "Now behave, we can do whatever we want with you, you are ours. Behave, or I will show you what you are going to have to do."

I wasn't sure what he meant, but I knew it would not be good. He threw me on the bed.

The door opened, Eric came in. He looked at my red face and the blood on my leg and said, "You don't have to be so mean to her, she will cooperate. Please don't hit her again." He said with some compassion, but then he said, "I don't want her damaged."

"I want her cleaned-up, dressed nice, make-up and looking like the girl we want when we return in the morning," the Caucasian man yelled at Eric, I'm not paying for a snip of a girl that thinks she can do whatever she wants. Make her behave, I don't care what it takes, beat her, drug her, whatever you have to do. I want to see a beautiful girl, not messy with blood all over her leg. Do you understand me?"

With that they all walked out and locked the door.

This couldn't be happening! Eric had warned these terrible men not to be mean to me, maybe he did care. It was all so confusing! Could I trust Eric or not? No, I told myself, I cannot trust him, he is my kidnapper. I can fight with all my might, if they kill me, so what! But Mia, please Lord, let Mia be safe. Eric is not my friend, he is a sadistic monster, and his mother is worse. I told myself all this as I limped around the room, looking for something, I didn't know what.

Charles Wu took a shower, then talked to Jim Travis again, telling him to please do his best to obtain the warrant and page him when he had it. He came back downstairs and found Jenny waiting, ready to go.

"Oh Dad," she said, "we have to get her out of that house today. I can't imagine what she is going through and little Mia."

"I agree; I'm working on a warrant. As soon as I get it, we will go in there with the SWAT team. I also told Jim to look into the cold case involving Eric's father's murder. I have always been convinced that Helen O'Malley was involved somehow. But first we are going to stop by the Ling Store and question them," he said.

When Charles and Jenny walked into the Ling store it was still a mess. Both Mr. and Mrs. Ling were busy cleaning up.

"Hi Mr. Ling," Charles said ignoring Mrs. Ling. "it looks like the quake hit you pretty hard."

"Yes," he answered. "But we almost have it cleaned up, there wasn't any structural damage, except for the stairs. We are luckier than a lot of people."

"I'm looking for Chan-lei and the baby," Charles said getting right to the point.

"Isn't she at your house, when she left she said that was where she was going, she wanted to be with your family," Mr. Ling said.

"No, she is missing. Tell me what she said and if there were anyone else around. I'm afraid she might have met with foul play."

Mrs. Ling walked over with her usual sour look.

"That spoiled brat was scared by the earthquake, she ran out with the baby and nothing else," Mrs. Ling said.

Jenny bristled with Mrs. Ling's remark and said:

"Mrs. Ling, you and I both know she wouldn't just run out like that. She was expecting me and if she had a choice she would have waited here for me. What did you say to her? And for your information, Chan-lei is anything but a spoiled brat."

Mrs. Ling was shocked by Jenny's tone but remained polite because she knew who Charles Wu was and she didn't want to anger a District Attorney.

"I don't know what to tell you Jenny, Mrs. Ling said softly. "She simply walked out, I don't know where she is."

"Was Eric O'Malley around?" Charles asked.

"Why no," Mrs. Ling answered innocently, "Why would you ask about Eric?"

Charles noticed Mrs. Ling looked frightened when he mentioned Eric. He felt she had something to hide.

"I have my reasons," he answered. "Now I need to look at Chan-lei's apartment."

Mrs. Ling showed them upstairs. The apartment was a mess, glass broken all over the floor. Jenny noticed the cake smashed on the floor and a tear came into her eye and she thought how clean and perfect Chan-lei always kept the apartment."

"We will be back to clean this up," Charles said. "Please don't touch anything. This is now part of a crime scene."

As Charles and Jenny walked out of the store, Mrs. Ling turned to help a customer and Mr. Ling followed them out to the street.

"My wife was not very nice to Chan-lei," he said. "She ordered her out, I'm so sorry. And shortly after she left, Eric O'Malley came in the store and my wife told him Chan-lei was walking to your house. I don't always understand my wife. Chan-lei is such a nice girl, I tried to warn her once about Eric. Please find her."

Jenny took Mr. Ling's hand and said, "We will find her, we will."

"If you hear anything, please call me," Charles said and handed him his card. "Day or night, please."

Jenny noticed tears in Mr. Ling's eyes.

TWENTY-ONE

AFTER THE MEN LEFT, I WENT TO THE BATHROOM and cleaned the blood off my leg and put a new bandage on it. I looked in the mirror and could see a bruise forming on my temple from when that terrible man had thrown me against the wall. The back of my head hurt and I could feel a large lump on it. I looked drawn and terrible, I hadn't had any sleep in what seemed like days. I washed my face with cold water and went to check on Mia, asleep on the bed. *What must she think of this?* I thought.

Everything was quiet again so I thought this was a good opportunity to try the window again. Traffic noise sounded on the street that might cover up and noise I might make. I looked at the window, and there was a crack in the corner. I started to work on making a hole, when I got a space big enough for both of us, I would make my escape. I looked for tweezers, thinking they might help, but no they did nothing. Chipping away with my hand, finally getting a small hole in the corner, I had to be careful not to cut myself and make any real noise. A shard of glass could be used as a weapon but so far I had little pieces at best.

I was feeling nauseous and dizzy so I pulled the heavy drapes over the window and sat down on the bed. I began to sweat and my mind seemed blurry.

My thoughts rushed up and collided. *I was never going to get out of here! Where were Jenny and the Wu's? Did they care? Was anyone looking for me? Where was Chi? Was he ever coming back? Maybe they would all forget me and move on with their lives. I wanted my mother, she would not forget me. Was she okay, did she know I had been kidnapped? Maybe, somehow I could get Mia to the Wu's and she would be safe, but how could I do that?* Tears ran down my face, and my heart pounded. *Please Lord, please, help me to get out of here,* I prayed.

Charles and Jenny drove to the O'Malley house where David was watching the house. He was tired and so happy to see them. They both got into David's car.

"I'm so happy you're back," he said "I was afraid of falling asleep. I had to keep pinching myself."

"So sorry I was gone so long," Charles said. "Jenny and I went to the Ling store to see if there were any clues there. I'm convinced Mrs. Ling had something to do with this, she lied to us. Mr. Ling said Eric had been there shortly after Chan-lei left."

"You won't believe what has been going on here," David said. "Three men arrived early this morning and stayed in the house for about forty-five minutes."

"What did they look like? Charles asked.

"Two were Chinese and one was white. They wore dark suits but looked burly, like thugs," David answered.

Probably the brokers," Charles said. "We have to get her out of here, my investigator is working on a warrant. Then I will go in with several police officers or the SWAT team, get her and arrest the O'Malley's. Has anyone left the house?

"No," David answered. "It was quiet until the men showed up."

Tears welled up in Jenny's eyes. "Oh poor Chan-lei, what are they doing to her and to Mia? Chan-lei is so sweet and innocent, we have to do something now, not just sit here doing nothing."

Charles looked frustrated and lashed out at Jenny, "Jenny, you have no idea how much I want to storm in there. But I can't barge into the house without a warrant. If I do, I will be the one arrested and I will lose my job. We have to wait here and watch and let my team do their work."

Jenny hugged her Dad and wished that he wasn't so ethical. But she also told herself she was glad he was the way he was.

No one came in my room all morning. I worked on the window until I had a decent size hole in it. I was careful because I didn't want to let any cold in, it was a foggy and cold day. I knew if it was cold in the room when they came back, they would know something was wrong. If they find the hole, they would hit me again or do something worse. I was on the backside of the house, if I screamed or made a big commotion, no one would hear me. I thought I would make a sling out of the sheet and wrap Mia in and tie it around me. Problem was, I had nothing to cut the sheet with. But I would find a way. I didn't want to do it too soon; afraid they would catch me. When it was time, I could break the entire window out and go through it fast. I had to have everything prepared before I could do this.

I went from feeling confident that I would make it out, to panic that I wouldn't. I felt hopeful and then felt sick. I would get dizzy and nauseated and then feel a little better. I had to get out soon. I whispered to Mia about our situation:

"We will be okay, little one. Daddy will come for us! We are strong, we will succeed in getting out of here. Don't worry, I will take care of you. I love you more than anyone in the world, I won't let anything happen to you. I will die before that happens."

I felt confident, but extremely scared, not sure if I could get Mia out. I was depressed at times thinking I should end it all and find a way to kill both myself and Mia, feeling it would be better than the alternative. They were taking us to Burma where I would be sold into prostitution and my love, Mia, would be raised to be a prostitute. My mind was playing tricks on me, one minute feeling I could get out and the next feeling defeated. I had to do something, I knew I couldn't kill Mia or myself. I had to get out!

Later that evening, Eric brought some Asian soup for me. I was hungry but I didn't want to eat.

"You must eat, Chan-lei," he said softly.

"Why," I said. "I would rather die of starvation then endure what you have in store for me."

"You will be okay; my mother will explain the life you will have. It will not be as bad as you think," he said.

"The only life I want is with Chi and Mia," I said coldly. "Please Eric, please understand."

"I'm sorry Chan-lei, you could have played it differently. I would have given you riches, but now you must give riches to me. You are beautiful, you are worth money."

"What are you talking about?" I said confused by his compliments and the dizziness in my head.

"You have the beauty they seek, young, slim girls are perfect for the brothels. You look even younger than you are, they will pay money for you, a lot of money."

"Please Eric, you know Chi and the Wu's will never stop looking for me."

"They will forget you," he said and turned to leave.

"They will never forget me or Mia," I shouted as he slammed the door.

I ate some of the soup because of Mia, although it was cold and tasteless. I need to eat and keep my energy up to nurse her. Feeling a little better, my head was not as dizzy after eating a little. After feeding Mia, I planned what to do next. I had to have a plan.

Stripping off the top sheet, I looked for a way to cut it. If only I could find scissors or a knife. As I looked toward the window, I realized there was a sharp piece of glass there. If I could hold the sheet and pull with both hands against the glass, I could make a cut and then tear the rest. It worked! The tearing made a sound but it couldn't be heard with all the noise on the street. Once the first strip was torn, it was much easier. I tore a large piece to make a sling and then smaller ones to tie around me. When I finished, I hid them under the mattress.

Sleeping was next to impossible that night. I kept waiting for those horrible men to return. I prayed most of the night. Charles and Jenny were watching outside, but I didn't know that. I felt abandoned.

Please Lord, please let me get Mia out of here. I don't even care about myself anymore, just Mia. Let her be found and saved.

It was late afternoon when Jim Travis arrived at the O'Malley house. He found Charles sitting in his car watching the house.

"Tim," Charles jumped when he walked up to his car. "Did you get the warrant signed?"

"No, I have nothing but bad news for you. The judge said since no one has seen the girl in the house, he cannot sign the warrant. He said she could be anywhere, she could be hurt in the earthquake, or run away on her own accord."

"But I know she is in there," Charles said with frustration. "They have her hidden, they are not going to parade her around outside. Judge Clark knows me; he knows I'm not hot headed. If they harm her, he will have to answer to me! I have been working on the missing girls' cases for years and finally I almost have proof of what I have suspected. And this isn't just any girl, Chan-lei is like a daughter to me, what if it was Jenny? "

Tim looked sad and mumbled, "I'm so sorry."

"Tim, we have to get a warrant. Try another judge or go to the District Attorney himself. I must get in there today; tomorrow will be too late."

Charles was angry, he had worked hard for many years and had prosecuted many cases. Judge Clark knew he was an excellent DA. Charles then talked to Jenny and David:

"Will you two be okay if I go to the office for a while in the morning? I'm going to plead with Judge Clark, we have to get Chan-lei and Mia out of there! We can take turns watching the house tonight, but we are all getting tired, and can't do this much longer. Jenny, I think you should get some sleep, I worry about you. And David, you too and then come back in the morning to relieve me."

"What if we see them take Chan-lei?" David asked.

Charles thought for a moment and then said:

"From now on, you and Jenny stay together. If you see them leave,

David you follow them. Jenny, you get to a phone and call me. I only wish we could spot her in the house, that would give me a warrant. I'm thinking of sneaking around the house when it gets darker and trying to see if I can spot her."

After Jenny and David left, Charles sat in the car planning what to do in the morning. First, he would go over the reports and investigations of the missing girls. Then he would review the Patrick O'Malley murder. There had to be something to convince Judge Clark to sign the warrant. What was missing? Time was running out!

TWENTY-TWO

I SLEPT FITFULLY, WAKING LONG BEFORE THE LIGHT. I must escape today, I thought. I can't stay here another day. Is there a weapon I can use? I considered killing them, but how? I must find a way to save Mia.

I laid next to the sleeping Mia and remembered how wonderful it was when Chi and I first arrived in San Francisco. We had so many plans, so much going our way. I went to school for a semester. And then our precious Mia was born, and our life seemed so perfect. My thoughts went to Chi and how much I had come to love him. Was his father still alive? Would they be joining us here in America? All this seemed a little moot considering I might not be alive to see them arrive, or if I did live, I would probably be a prostitute in Burma. Why was I attracted to Eric when we were first here? He turned out to be the worse of the worse, and his mother, she was so menacing, she had made Eric the monster he is. Today I would get out that window! They cannot have Mia, there is no way. Was I being punished for my feelings for Eric so long ago? I said a prayer and asked God to please forgive me.

Please Lord, forgive me for my sin of looking at another man. You gave me Chi and I promise to never betray him in any way. Please keep Mia safe and help us get out of here, back to Chi. But most of all, please forgive me."

As soon as David and Jenny returned, Charles went home and told his wife everything that was going on. He slept for a short time and then showered and left for his office.

When he walked in the office, Tim was there.

"I'm going to go through the discovery on both the girls' cases and the O'Malley murder case. I must find something to make Judge Clark sign that warrant. If not, I'm going to every judge in the region. I don't think we have any more time left."

"I'm so sorry I didn't get it yesterday, Charles. What can I do to help?"

Later, Jenny went back to the Wu house. Dr. Wu was there and worried. Jenny hugged her, started to cry and asked what she should do. She trusted her mother to give advice more than anyone else on earth.

"I think you should write an affidavit on how Eric shows up

wherever you and Chan-lei are. Also put in the affidavit what Chan-lei told you about seeing him other places and the car following her. I'm not sure, but that may help your father get his warrant," Dr. Wu said.

"I never thought of that," Jenny said. "Mom you might make a better attorney than I ever will."

"I will leave the law to you and your father," Dr. Wu laughed. "I'll stick to medicine, which reminds me, I need to be at the hospital. Many were hurt in the quake and several deaths. Did you hear the freeways collapsed and the damage to the Bay Bridge? Thank God our neighborhood survived with a small amount of damage."

Dr. Wu went to the hospital and Jenny started to write an affidavit. She would take it to her father's office and have them type it. If it needed changes, they could do it there.

The morning was dragging by, no one brought me food or came to check on me. The window opening was as big as it could be before I broke it out completely and escaped. I looked for something to smash the window quickly. Maybe a dresser drawer? Just when I was going to prepare the sling the door opened.

Helen O'Malley came in carrying several things.

"I brought you some bath things and clean underwear. I want you to bathe and wash your hair. I will be back to dress you, fix your hair, and do your makeup. You must look exceptionally pretty today," she said.

"Why?" I said.

"The brokers are coming to set your price. The prettier you look the more money I will get. I want them to see a beautiful woman, not some disheveled little girl."

With that remark, she put the items she carried down and quickly left the room. I looked at what she had brought, nice smelling soap, bath salts, lotion and deodorant. Along with underwear and a cotton robe. But nothing heavy that I could break the window with.

With a heavy heart I filled the tub.

Chi was finally allowed to see his father. He looked pale with a breathing tube in and not awake. The nurse told him he would wake up soon but Chi was very worried. His father looked so ill, and there was nothing he could do for him, but be there. He was so worried about his wife and daughter, where could they be? He sat down next to his father's bed. Soon his mother came in and Chi pulled another chair up to the bed for her. They sat holding hands.

"Mama, you do understand that I need to get back to Chan-lei as soon as possible. I'm very worried about her and Mia," Chi said seriously.

"My son, I realize this. Your home is now in America with your wife and daughter, I will be okay here with your father," she said sadly.

I'm sad to leave you but as soon as Father recovers you have a home in America also," Chi told her.The door opened and the doctor walked in.

"The surgery went very well and barring any complications, he will recover nicely. He will have to make changes in his diet, but we will discuss this before he leaves the hospital," he said to both of them.

"I have to return to America right away," Chi said. "There has been an earthquake and my wife and daughter are in danger," Chi replied.

"Your father will be okay for now, you can leave. Please, you need to go to your wife and daughter. Do not worry," he said with compassion.

"My husband and I are also moving to American as soon as we can," Mrs. Wah added.

"It will be a few weeks, maybe a month or more before Mr. Wah can travel," he said back.

Chi told his mother that as soon as his father was awake he had to leave and find a flight back to San Francisco. His mother agreed, being worried about her daughter-in-law and granddaughter. She held a photograph of Mia that Chi had brought her.

I got out of the tub and put the underwear and robe on. I couldn't believe how well it fit. How did Mrs. O'Malley know my sizes or did she guess? Mia was sleeping on the bed. I had left the bathroom door open so I could see her and make sure no one came in.

In a few short minutes, Mrs. O'Malley came back in the room carrying a red dress on a hanger, a pair of high heel shoes, a plastic box that looked like a little suitcase, two bottles of wine and two glasses. She put them in the bathroom, went back in the hall and picked up a chair. She sat the chair in the bathroom and ordered me to sit down.

I looked at the chair and hoped she would leave it in the room when she left. I could break the entire window out fast with the chair.

"Now I will transform you into a beauty," she said. "Would you like a glass of wine while we work?"

"No, thank you," I said, "I don't drink wine."

"Well then, it is time you start," she said and poured wine in the glasses.

I sat down and she produced a hair dryer and began to dry my hair. As she did, she took several drinks of the wine and started to talk to me.

"You know, Chan-lei, this will not be such a bad life for you. You will actually live in luxury. You will have beautiful clothes, jewels, and men catering to your every need," she said.

"All I need or want is Chi and Mia," I said.

She took another drink of the wine. "Don't worry, you will find life will be good, always beautiful clothes, jewels and accommodations. When you grow too old, you will be taken care of with love and respect. So much better than being the wife of a common cook."

"Chi is not a cook," I said back, "he is a chef! And I want nothing else but to be his wife. He will own his own restaurant soon and I will be a lawyer. We have a bright future ahead of us and it does not include selling myself."

Mrs. O'Malley laughed and took another drink of the wine. "I don't think you understand your future," she said. "Listen to me, you will not be a usual prostitute in a rundown brothel, you will have riches, and be adored by many men. You will be a courtesan, not a prostitute, and you will soon forget your life as it is now."

"What is a courtesan?"

She took another drink of wine and seemed to think for a moment. "A courtesan is different from a prostitute or whore; the word is from the French. A courtesan gives pleasure to men, but is also courted and admired by wealthy men. She is wined and dined, given gifts and sometimes loved by very successful men. She lives a life of luxury. Oh, I thought about this career many times. Now drink your wine, it will relax you."

I took a sip, but it tasted bitter and I didn't like it. I took another sip, maybe it would give me courage.

Mia woke up and Mrs. O'Malley told me to shut her up. I went to the bed and picked her up then sat back down with her on my lap.

"You keep that child quiet, I don't want any noise," she said impatiently.

I picked up where the conversation had ended. "So why didn't you choose the life of a courtesan, if it is all that wonderful? I asked.

"Because I married young and had Eric. By the time I learned of that life it was too late for me, but it is not too late for you. Have another drink," she said with a smirk. I put the glass to my lips but only took a tiny sip, maybe I could make her believe I was drinking it.

"But I am married and have a child," I said.

"That doesn't matter now, my dear," she said.

"Tell me about your husband, Mrs. O'Malley," I said with a little trepidation.

"What do you want to know about him and why?" she answered with restraint.

"What was he like? What made you want to marry him? What kind of a father was he?"

I was suddenly full of questions. What could she do? She wouldn't hit me again and mess up the merchandise.

She laughed her rather sinister laugh and said, "Oh, he was a very handsome man and really loved me at first. He gave me gifts and promised me the moon. He was happy when Eric was born, but everything changed. He became more focused on Eric than me. He didn't like it when I went out with my friends, he wanted me to stay home and take care of Eric."

I played along to find out all I possibly could about this woman. I thought to myself that I would make a good investigator.

"I can understand that," I said a little timid. "Chi is like that, he wants me to be the perfect wife and mother but I want to go to law school but he just wants a housewife."

Oh please let her believe me, I prayed. *And forgive me for disrespecting my husband. I need to find out things from this woman.*

"So you decided to divorce him?" I said knowing I was stepping on dangerous ground.

"Yes, but he was an expert at family law and I was afraid he would get sole custody of Eric. In those days' custody almost always went to the mother, but he knew too much about me and also knew the right judges. I was afraid to lose my son; I couldn't let that happen. You see, I was not always the perfect wife."

She picked up the corkscrew and opened the second bottle of wine. She had drunk the first bottle and didn't seem to notice that I was not drinking.

Mia squirmed on my lap and Mrs. O'Malley raised the hair brush like she was going to hit her. I held Mia closer and patted her, she settled down. I wondered what kind of a mother she had been when Eric was a baby.

She worked on my hair, putting it up in a bun of sorts and decorating it with Chinese combs. She stood back, looked at my hair and smiled. She seemed satisfied and turned my face toward her and began putting on makeup, something I never wore. She painted my eyelids with shadow and then lined my eyes with black. She drank more of the wine.

"So what did you do next?" I said with caution trying to get her back into the conversation.

"Nothing," she answered.

She seemed to be in deep thought for a while, and worked on putting red stuff on my cheeks with a brush.

I was working at being an investigator. It seemed to come natural to me. Gain her confidence, make her believe Chi was like Patrick, and she will tell me what I want to know. Easy.

"Did you file for divorce?" I asked.

"Oh no," she answered. "I was afraid Patrick would win in the courts. He knew everyone in the legal system and had an excellent record of being an ethical attorney. They would all believe him, not me."

"So what did you do? I pressed with little caution now.

"What would you do?" she asked and drank more of the wine.

"I know I would do anything and I mean anything not to lose my child. Mia means more to be than anyone else in this world." I answered as I held Mia a little closer.

I looked down at my baby and she looked at me being very still. Did she somehow comprehend the danger she was in?

"That is exactly how I felt," she said sadly. "I couldn't lose my Eric, no matter what I had to do."

I felt she was telling the truth. She didn't seem to pick up on my statement that I would do anything to save my child.

"Mrs. O'Malley," I started, "I understand, I really do. I will do anything to save my baby. I know Eric likes me, if he wants me, I will be his mistress. I will love and care for him and make him happy. But I need to know Mia will be safe. I will leave Chi or stay with him and see Eric when I can, whatever you want me to do." I was desperate again pleading.

"That is not a choice anymore Chan-lei," she said. "You had your chance and you chose Chi. Eric told me, but don't despair, you will have a good life, one filled with riches. You will not have to be married to a chef and have baby after baby."

She had finished with the makeup and drank the rest of the wine in the bottle.

She pointed to the dress hanging on the shower door. "Put this dress on," she said, "they will be here soon."

"Okay," I answered "but please tell me how you got out of the situation with Eric's father, what really happened?"

She had drunk two bottles of wine and her words had begun to slur and I needed to keep her talking. I looked in the mirror and couldn't believe what I saw. I didn't look anything like myself. What I saw was a woman, not a girl, with eye makeup making my eyes look larger, pink streaks across my cheeks, bright red lipstick. I didn't look beautiful, I looked like a *Jinu,* a Chinese whore. I stared at the reflection and knew I must try anything to get free. I glanced over at the wine bottles, maybe I could hit her with one.? What about the corkscrew? Could I stab her with it? But if I didn't knock her out or disable her, she could hurt Mia.

"Put the little brat down and get into this dress," she said now really slurring her words.

I carefully laid Mia on the bed, put the dress on and turned so she could zip it up. "So, tell me what you did to get free of your husband," I was now taking chances, I knew. I was shocked and amazed with she answered very coldly:

"I had him killed, it was the only thing I could do."

My heart seemed to stop and then started pumping very hard.

"What? How? I cried out.

"Easy. I met a man and he told me it was simple," she said with no emotion. "I paid him a lot of money, and he told me it could never be linked to me, a quick break-in robbery and I would have it all." she looked at me and became cruel. She realized what she had said.

"You make sure you never tell anyone what I just told you. If you do, I will deny it, no one will believe you anyway, and I will make sure that baby of yours suffers great pain before she dies. You will also die and so will your husband and the entire Wu family. Be aware that I can make this happen."

She was not just slurring her words, she now seemed unsteady on her feet. I felt frozen, she had threatened to not only kill me, but do worse to my baby. I had to play along with her until I could escape, I had to save my baby. This was the time to act, hit her with the wine bottle and then escape out the window while she was unconscious. I reached for one of the wine bottles.

Suddenly the door opened and Eric came in with the same three men from yesterday.

TWENTY-THREE

THE THREE MEN WERE THE SAME AS BEFORE, but they looked at me differently. They seemed surprised as to how I looked now. I had withdrawn my hand from the wine bottle and ran over to the bed to protect Mia. The horrible man that had hit me before followed me.

"You finally look like you are supposed to, but don't do anything stupid or this time it will be your baby that I hurt," he said quietly but sternly.

"Please do not touch my baby," I said. "she has done nothing to you, you have no reason to hurt her. I will cooperate with you."

He took a hold of my face with one hand squeezing it hard. Pain shot through my jaw.

"Remember what you said, you will cooperate with us!" he said and let go.

The other two men walked over and looked me up and down. *I have never seen such evil people,* I thought to myself. *I must go along with them until I have a chance to escape. It must be when they leave, if they leave. What if they take me right now?*

They turned me around and looked at me from every angle. I felt like a piece of meat, not a person. Panic started to overtake me again, but I couldn't let it. I felt sick, but suppressed the urge to vomit and looked down.

"We will agree to the price you asked for," the Caucasian man said to Eric. "We will be back tonight after dark, have her ready. The ships are being allowed to leave the harbor now after the quake and we have a ship that has agreed to take her. She can take the baby with her or not, but we will not pay extra. She will cost us money to care for her until she is of age. If you have a buyer for the baby, I suggest you take it."

"She will be ready," was all Eric said.

One of the Asian men came over to me and said: "Be prepared for an interesting voyage little girl. I'm going with you and I will teach you how to pleasure men on the trip. By the time we arrive you will not be so feisty. If you do not cooperate, I will beat or drug you, do as I say or suffer the consequences."

"And remember, if you have the baby with you, it will also be her that suffers," the Caucasian man said and raised his hand to hit me. I tried not to flinch but couldn't help it. He laughed.

With that. as fast as they had walked in, they walked out. I noticed Eric gave his mother a strange look, did he realize she was drunk?

In a couple of minutes, Mrs. O'Malley came back in.

"Get my beautiful dress off," she said. "I will be back with something for you to wear tonight. It won't be like this dress, but you will need decent clothes to wear on the journey," she laughed and was still slurring her words.

They talked about taking Mia from me. This could not happen. I had to act quickly. I only had until dark or before.

Jenny walked into her father's office. He was surprised, she was supposed to stay with David.

"What are you doing here," he said "You should not leave David alone, this is a critical day."

"I know Dad, but Mom and I thought if I gave you an affidavit of what has been going on with Eric, always showing up where Chan-lei is, it would help get a warrant. So I wrote this and thought we could have it typed and I will sign it. I'll get back to David as soon as possible."

"That is very smart of you, you might make a great lawyer," he said as he glanced over the paper.

"Actually it was Mom's idea," Jenny said.

"Your Mom is very smart, and so are you Jenny," he winked at her.

The affidavit was printed and signed in a very short time. Jenny left to go back to David and Charles was on his way to Judge Clark.

As soon as they left, I jumped into action not sure when Mrs. O'Malley would be back with the clothes. I tore off the dress and put on the robe, having nothing else to wear. I pulled the strips out from under the mattress. I learned to make a sling for a baby in one of my classes in China. I tied the ends together tight so they would not come apart with Mia's weight. Pulling it over my head I opened it up and put Mia in it. She was being so quiet, and fitted in the sling nicely. I took the strips of the sheet and tied them around us so Mia couldn't fall out when I climbed out the window. I glanced at the wine bottles, picked one up and put it under the robe and one of the strips held it tight. I didn't want to put it in the sling, afraid I could fall and it might cut Mia. It was okay if it cut me.

"Okay, my precious little girl, this is it. Remember if it all goes wrong; I love you more than anyone in the world. If it goes right, I promise never to put you in danger ever again. I'm so sorry you are going through this." I whispered to Mia.

I heard Eric and his mother arguing outside of the door. He sounded mad. I had to hurry before they came in here.

"You have to keep your wits, Mother. This is almost over and we can't have any mistakes. Chan-lei is smarter than any of the other girls. What is wrong with you," he said.

"I'm sorry Eric, I was enjoying dressing her up and talking to her and I didn't realize how much wine I drank, I wanted her to drink it," Mrs. O'Malley said.

"No more, we have to have her ready soon. They will bring the money when they come for her. We need it. Find clothes for her to wear now," Eric said.

I couldn't hear any more, so I went to the window and looked out. Although we were on the second floor it didn't look all that far to the ground. Even if I fell, we might be hurt but it wouldn't kill us. If I could reach the trellis with my foot we could climb down it, but I had to be quick. I didn't have shoes, but I could do it with bare feet.

My knee was painful, even more so than before, but I had to ignore it and do what I had to do. When we got to the ground, I would crawl or whatever I had to do to get to the street and then cause as big a commotion as possible.

I went in the bathroom; the chair was there where she had left it. I picked it up. Now with a little luck, I would be free.

The minute Jenny left the office, Charles attached the affidavit to the warrant and headed to Judge Clark's chambers. He walked in just as the judge was leaving the bench for a recess.

"James, can I have a moment with you?" Charles asked.

"Yes, of course, Charles, but I don't think I can sign that warrant," he said.

"Please, listen to me for a moment. You are a fair judge and you also know I'm not some hotheaded DA that wouldn't carefully consider everything before asking for a warrant."

"Okay, tell me your reasons for the emergency," he said Charles started his argument as Judge Clark looked over the affidavit.

"I have another young Chinese girl missing from Chinatown. She is not just any girl; she is a friend of my daughter. My family has become very close to this girl since she arrived from China a year ago, she has been followed repeatedly by Eric O'Malley as the affidavit states. Everywhere Chan-lei, the girl, goes Eric shows up and when she doesn't see him, she sees his car. Chan-lei has been missing since the earthquake and this is out of character for her. She is married and has a baby, her husband was called to China for a medical emergency with his father. The baby hopefully is with her, I've been watching the O'Malley house and men have visited. Eric went out and bought diapers. Your Honor, I know this girl, she is a kind, innocent girl. Please, I'm begging you, we must save her."

Judge Clark saw a tear in Charles' eye as he picked up a pen and signed the warrant.

Jenny returned to David. As she slid into the car he said:

"They were here again, those men. This time they didn't stay very long, looked in a hurry then they left. I think they plan to take her soon."

"Oh no, poor Chan-lei," Jenny said. Jenny returned to David. As she slid into the car he said:

"When I saw them go in the house, I was afraid they would come out with her. I didn't know what to do, should I run up to them and make a big commotion and maybe the neighbors would call the cops and I was also afraid they would shoot me," David said letting his frustration out.

"My fear would be that they would hurt her or Mia, but I think you're right, we can't let them take her," Jenny said.

"I'm not sure what we should do, but we need a plan," David said.

"I don't think they will bring her out the front door," Jenny said sadly. "But if they do, we should do what you said about a big commotion. But if a car leaves the garage, we follow it, and maybe run into it, causing an accident and commotion."

"We have to do something Jenny, I feel so helpless. I don't think I'm very good at this detective business," David replied.

Jenny leaned over and gave him a kiss on the cheek and a hug:

"I think you are good at everything," she said.

I could hardly believe how good and quiet Mia was. It was almost like she knew what was happening and had to be quiet. I patted her gently and kissed the top of her head. Now was the time, I couldn't wait a second more. They would be back anytime. I checked the sling to make sure it was right, hoping it would hold Mia when I climbed out the window. I thought of Chi. As I picked up the chair I said a prayer:

Please dear Lord, let this work and let Mia and I escape from this nightmare. Keep her safe above all else. If I fall, please don't let her be hurt and if you can't save me, please save her. Keep Chi safe and let his father be well. Again, I'm sorry for my sins. Let Chi, my parents, and the Wu's know how much I love them all."

With the signed warrant in hand, Charles called the San Francisco Police Department and told them to have uniformed officers meet him at the O'Malley house. Then he called his wife:

"Hi Honey, I want you to know I have the warrant, thanks to you and Jenny. I'm on my way with the SFPD."

"Oh Charles, please save that sweet girl and her baby but also keep yourself safe. I can barely think of what Chan-lei is going through. When this is over, we may never let them out of our sight," Dr. Wu said.

"I feel the same, now I must meet the SFPD and get our girl."

"Be safe," she said.

Charles ran to his car to serve the most important warrant of his career.

I gave Mia one more little kiss, picked up the chair and hit the window. Glass shattered, it made a noise but not as loud as I thought it would. I picked out a couple of large jagged pieces of the glass. Pain went through my knee, and I felt lightheaded but I had to ignore the pain and do what I had to do. I lifted my leg over the window sill and just as I did Mia let out a scream and I felt a hand grab the back of my neck.

"Where do you think you are going?"

I turned around to see steel blue eyes. **Eric!**

Shirley Nolan

TWENTY-FOUR

"IF THAT BLUE-EYED CHINESE BASTARD HAS HURT THEM, I will kill him with my bare hands." Chi sat in an airport chair waiting to be called for his flight back to San Francisco. He was on stand-by and so nervous he was shaking. Fearing the plane would be full and he would have to wait for another flight, his hands shook and he dabbed at a tear. He started pacing then, he couldn't sit still. So afraid he may never see his precious wife and daughter again, he walked over to a bank of phones and placed a call to the Wu home.

"Dr. Wu," he said nervously when she answered, this is Chi Wah. Is there any news?"

"Yes Chi," she answered. "Charles has a warrant and is on his way to the O'Malley house right now. If Chan-lei and Mia are in that house, he will save them. We are almost positive she is there. Where are you? How is your father? Has Chan-lei tried to call you per chance? She flooded him with questions.

"Oh thank God," he said. "I'm at the airport, on stand-by, waiting for the next flight. If I can't get on this flight, I will call you back in about a half-hour. But if I make it I will not be able to call until I reach San Francisco. I'm praying by that time, my wife and daughter will be safe. And to answer your other question, my father is doing well. And I have heard nothing from my wife.,"

"Good news about your father, Chi. Call as soon as you land in San Francisco. Do you want me to send Jenny to meet you?" Dr. Wu said.

"Thank you but no, I will take a cab to your house. Jenny is needed there. Dr. Wu, I can't thank you enough for what you and Mr. Wu are doing to find my family," Chi said.

"Oh Chi, you and Chan-lei mean so much to us. I'm praying I have good news for you when you call again," she said.

Chi hung up the phone and paced some more, hoping Chan-lei was being rescued at this moment. He sat back down when he heard over the PA system:

"Will Mr. Chi Wah please come to the desk at Gate 32." He was on the flight.

Jenny and David sat in the car feeling as nervous as cats, drinking coffee that Jenny had brought back with her.

"Please pray Dad gets that warrant," Jenny said. "I know she is in there; we have to get her out."

Jenny's hands shook as she leaned over to pick up the paper cup of coffee and it spilled all over her.

"Oh David, I'm so jumpy I can't hold on to a cup of coffee without spilling it," Jenny cried.

"It's okay Honey, I'm the same," David said handing her a napkin that was tucked between the seats. "Honestly, I don't know how your Dad does it, I don't like this at all. I would make a poor investigator."

"You are a great investigator," Jenny replied. "I'm a nervous wreck but I think this is what I want to do, save people from evil and prosecute the bad guys. But you are probably better off sticking with computer programing."

David thought that even in this serious situation, Jenny was an upbeat pixie. He realized that he had fallen in love with her, and her family as well.

All of a sudden four police cars screeched to a halt in front of the house and Jenny saw her Dad running up to the car.

"You two stay put, I don't want you hurt," he instructed Jenny and David. "I have my warrant, thanks to you, Jenny."

He ran toward the house as the police joined him.

The hand on the back of my neck was ice cold. I whirled around as Eric was screaming at me:

"Don't think you are going to escape, you little bitch," he screamed. "Your fate is already sealed." He raised his hand to strike me.

Without thinking, I held tight to Mia while I reached in my robe and pulled out the wine bottle. In a flash of an eye, I struck him, hitting his forehead. Eric let out what sounded like a cry from an animal and crumpled to the floor, his hands going to his head. I watched as bright red blood ran down his face. I wasn't sure if he was unconscious or not, but I knew even if he was, it would not be for long. The room was spinning and bile rose in my throat, but I had to suppress it.

I dropped the bottle, ran for the door and out into the hallway. Mia was screaming! Mrs. O'Malley ran up the stairs. I felt I was in a fog, everything was blurry. As I reached the top of the stairs, she reached out to grab me. The stairs were different from when they had brought me in here, they were wide and curved, made of a hard surface, maybe marble. Not carpeted like the other stairs, it was remarkable that I could think this in the state I was in.

"What did you do to my Eric? I heard him cry out," she yelled looking fuzzy to me. "If you hurt him, you will suffer before I kill you."

I didn't consider what I was doing, everything was by instinct. I raised my foot as high as I could and it landed in the middle of her stomach. I ignored the pain I felt in my leg. I was in another world, everything seemed to happening in slow motion. Pain ran from my thigh to my ankle, I couldn't believe how much pain. I watched as she seemed to be in shock and swayed a couple of times, losing her balance and toppling down the stairs. What took seconds, seemed to be an eternity.

I watched in horror as she tumbled down the stairs, rolling head over heels, like a rag doll, over and over, landing on the hard marble floor with a loud thud.

"You can't stop me," I shouted.

I felt like tumbling to the floor but not giving into the pain I ran down the stairs and by some miracle I didn't fall. Nothing seemed real, like I was in some foggy dream.

She was yelling, "My back, you broke my back. I will get you for this."

Eric ran down the stairs covered with blood and ran to his mother.

"Mother, what did she do to you?"

I ran to the door; it was a large double door with four or five locks on it. My hands were shaking as I fumbled with each lock. Three were simple deadbolts but the last one was complicated and had a key in it. As I fumbled with the lock Eric was coming for me.

"I will get you, you can't get away from me," he yelled. "You are going to pay for this, you are nothing but a jinu."

"She killed your father," I shouted back, "she is the one that will pay."

The key turned and the door opened. Standing on the entry walk was a sea of blue, police, all with guns drawn and Mr. Wu, also with a gun. At the same time, I felt both relief and pain running through my body. Mia was crying as loud as she possible could.

I hobbled to Mr. Wu, holding Mia in the sling tight to me, trying not to fall. He reached out with his arms open and the police ran past us into the house.

I fell into his welcoming arms, leaning into him and whispered, "she had Patrick O'Malley killed," and then my world went dark.

Jenny and David were watching from the car. When Jenny saw Chan-lei run out of the house she forgot what her father had said about staying in the car. All reason left her as she bolted out of the car towards Chan-lei. David sat with a shocked look on his face. *That's my Jenny,* he said out loud.

"Dad, Dad," Jenny yelled as she ran to them. "Is she hurt?'

"Jenny, untie the baby from Chan-lei and take her. I will take care of Chan-lei."

"Why is she unconscious? Is she dead? Jenny cried as she freed Mia and held her trying to comfort the hysterical baby.

"She is not dead, she fainted, I think," Charles said. "She is also burning with fever; we must get her to a hospital or your mother immediately."

"Mom," Jenny said, "she needs Mom, the hospitals are so full from the earthquake victims. Mom will take care of her."

One of the police officers came up to Charles. "We need an ambulance, the woman is badly hurt, and the man has a nasty cut on his head." He looked at an unconscious Chan-lei and said, "This little girl did some damage in there."

"Go and tell David to get to a phone and call your mother. Have him tell her Chan-lei is hurt, and we need her right now. You must bring Mia and come with me. I will tell you one thing, Chan-lei is one brave girl."

TWENTY-FIVE

I FELT ROCKING LIKE WHEN I WAS ON THE SHIP coming to America. Oh no, was I on a ship again? Was escaping all a dream? Was I on my way to Burma? Where was Mia? Did they take her from me? I felt panicky again. My eyelids fluttered but I couldn't open them. If I am on a ship and they have taken my baby, I will find a way to jump overboard, no way will I live the life they had planned for me.

I fought to open my eyes, and finally they slowly opened. I looked around, this was not a ship, it was a bedroom. Is it Eric's bedroom? Where is Mia? Where am I? I felt a light touch on my hand, when I turned to look, it was Chi. Was I dreaming?

"Chan-lei, my guingren, you are awake," Chi said in a whisper. He used the Chinese word for sweetheart.

"Where am I? Where is Mia?" I said in a panic, but relieved to see Chi next to me.

"At Dr. Wu's house, you have been very ill, she is caring for you. Mia is with Jenny, she is fine," Chi reassured me.

"Oh Chi, I thought I would never see you again," I started to cry.

The door opened and Jenny walked in with Mia in her arms. What a glorious sight! Jenny turned around and called out the door:

"Mom, she is awake, come here."

Dr. Wu came in with a big smile on her face.

"Welcome back Chan-lei," she said with such compassion. "You have been through a terrible time and have been ill, but you are back with us now. You will be better in no time."

She walked over to the bed, put her hand on my wrist, taking my pulse.

"Very good," she said, "do you want something to eat?"

"Just a drink of water," I said. "And can I hold my baby?"

Jenny brought Mia over to me and although I was very weak, I held her for a few minutes. She looked into my eyes like she remembered what we had been through.

"What happened to me? I said "All I remember is running out the door and seeing Mr. Wu there."

"We will tell you how brave you were after you get a little rest," Dr. Wu said. "You have a very serious cut on your knee and it caused an infection that traveled through your entire body. I cleaned the wound and stitched it up and I'm giving you strong antibiotics for the infection, they seem to be working. The vertigo, dizziness you feel is from both the infection and the antibiotics. It will dissipate as the antibiotics work on the infection."

"Good," I said. "I thought I was on a ship again, I thought they had me."

Chi leaned over and kissed my forehead. "They didn't get you to the ship," he said, "I don't know how you did it, but you got away from them."

"We were watching the house the entire time," Jenny said. "Dad will be home soon and he will tell you what happened after you fainted."

I smiled and then closed my eyes and went back to sleep.

I wasn't sure how long I slept, but when I woke up I felt much better. Chi was still sitting next to me. I noticed Mia's cradle at the end of the bed.

"Chi, how did the cradle get here?"

"Jenny and Dr. Wu went over to the apartment to get some of your things. They thought you would want the cradle." Chi said. "The apartment is a mess from the earthquake, but you never have to go back there. We will move into the new house as soon as you are well enough. Right now, all you have to worry about is getting well."

"Your father? How is he?

"He is doing okay, weak from the surgery, but will recover. I talked to my mother a little while ago, and she said he is in good spirits. They are both relieved to hear you and Mia are safe. I also talked to your parents, they are so happy you are safe. They will be leaving China in a few days."

"I can't wait to see them," I said. "What happened to Eric and Mrs. O'Malley."

"Mr. Wu will tell you about them, but they have been arrested," Chi answered.

I gave a sigh of relief. "I hope they spend a long time in prison, Chi, they were so mean to me and Mrs. O'Malley threatened to hurt Mia, to make her suffer. They are very bad people, very bad."

Jenny came in with some soup for me. It tasted so good, not like the bland soup I had been given by my captors. This was delicious. I could sit up now, and the dizziness didn't seem as bad.

"Dad will be home soon, he has quite a story to tell you, but I will let him tell it," Jenny said.

"I can't wait to hear it, and I have a lot to tell him. Jenny, thank you so much for all you did. I thought for a while I had been forgotten, but I should have known better," I said.

"We would never forget you, silly girl," Jenny replied.

I ate and then held Mia for a while. Jenny and Dr. Wu fixed a bottle of formula for Mia, I had never fed her with a bottle before, but she seemed to like it and drank it all.

"Mom says you shouldn't nurse her with the infection you have and the antibiotics you are taking," Jenny explained.

"I trust your mother, she is an excellent doctor," I smiled.

Mia was so content, she seemed to know we were safe now. I said a silent prayer to thank God we were safe.

Later that evening Mr. Wu knocked on my door and asked if he could come in.

"Of course," I said.

"It is good to see you awake," he said. "I was worried about you."

"I'm so much better Mr. Wu and I can't thank you enough for saving my life." I said.

"I think you saved yourself, Chan-lei," he said. "Eric has twenty-two stitches in his face and Mrs. O'Malley has a broken vertebra. She will recover, but it will be a while. You are the strongest little person I have ever known. And by the way, I think it is time you called me Charles," he said.

"They were going to take Mia from me, I had to do something." I said.

"And that you did," he smiled. "Now tell me how you know Mrs. O'Malley had her husband killed."

"She was fixing me up for those men and while she was doing my hair and makeup she drank a lot of wine. I kept talking to her about Eric and his father.

She was talking about how Patrick was going to take Eric away from her. She got mad at one point and blurted out that she hired someone to kill him. She said it was her only choice."

"That is what I thought all along," Charles said. "Now tell me about the men that came to visit you."

"They were very mean. Two were Asian and one was white. They threatened me and Mia. One hit me so hard I flew against the wall. They also said they would kill Mia If I didn't cooperate with them," I told him.

Chi was sitting quietly listening.

"Oh, Chan-lei, you have been through too much. I feel so bad that I had to leave you. I should have stayed here and you wouldn't have had to go through all this," Chi said as tears ran down his face.

"Chi," Charles said, "it is not your fault. Eric has been stalking Chan-lei for a long time. He would have kidnapped her eventually even if you were here. He used the earthquake to do his evil deed. Be thankful that you have such a strong wife. Who would guess that such a tiny girl could be so strong. You are a lucky man."

"I always knew she was strong but I never knew how strong," Chi said. "And I'm thankful we have good friends that looked out for her and Mia."

'Chan-lei, we also have arrested Mrs. Ling. She has been finding girls for Eric for years now. She pointed you out to Eric," Charles said.

"Oh, poor Mr. Ling," I said.

"Yes, I don't believe he knew. He is naïve and his wife, how do I say this, had the upper hand in the relationship. He knew she was up to no good, but he thought maybe she was selling drugs for Eric, which is also a crime that he should have reported but I feel sorry for him. He told me he tried to warn you about Eric," Charles said.

The note, I thought.

'I have always felt a little sorry for him," I said "He is so nice to me. I think I know how he tried to warn me, I will tell you later, I'm not sure if it is what he meant," I said feeling sorry for Mr. Ling.

"I don't think there will be any charges against him," Charles said. Now I'm going to investigate Patrick's murder. I have a lead from a man who was in a bar way back then and overheard Mrs. O'Malley talking to some guy and giving him an envelope that looked like it contained money, but he couldn't be sure. I have no idea how they overlooked this in the first investigation. If I can find this man, with his testimony and yours maybe we can file murder charges against her. I need to find him, because now it is just a rumor."

I was feeling very tired again, and Charles picked up on this and went downstairs. Chi joined him and I fell back to sleep.

When I woke up it was morning and I was alone in the room. On the bedside table sat the black box we had saved the cradle money in, a bowl of lotus blossoms and a note from Chi:

Jenny, David and I have gone to clean the apartment and move all our belongings to the new house. I will be back as soon as possible. Dr. Wu is taking care of Mia.

Rest and don't worry about anything. I love you more than you know.

Love, Chi

I felt so much better. I got out of bed and was surprised when I could walk without limping. There was a robe on the foot of the bed, I put it on and went looking for Mia.

I found both Mia and Dr. Wu in the kitchen. Mia was in her little carrier watching Dr. Wu make a pot of tea.

"Oh Chan-lei," Dr. Wu said. "Are you feeling better?"

"Oh yes," I smiled. I feel so much better. I think I can be of some use around her now."

"I want you to rest for a couple more days. The antibiotics are working but you still need time to recover."

"I can't thank you enough for what you have done for us," I cried.

"Please, don't think about it. We all love you. Jenny and Chi are cleaning out your apartment. I took the morning off to enjoy little Miss Mia here. They will be back soon. The nice thing is you will never have to go back to that apartment. They will move

242

everything to your new home. Charles is at work; he says he can't wait for you to join him at the DA's office."

"I'm not sure about that," I answered. "I think Chi will want me to stay home with Mia and not go to school, especially after all this."

"He may have second thoughts about that," she said with a wink. "Now, what can I fix you for breakfast?"

When Chi returned, he was surprised to find me in the kitchen with Dr. Wu.

"You look much better, Chan-lei," he said.

"I'm feeling better, still a bit tired and my knee is sore but I can help you move our things," I said.

"Oh no, you are not going to do anything but rest and eat until you are fully recovered. You lost weight and we have to fatten you up," he said with a joking smile.

"I'm sure that won't take much time," I said.

"Speaking of your knee, Chan-lei, Dr. Wu said seriously. "I did the best job I could to sew up that nasty cut. It had been several days and had a bad infection in it and I took out several pieces of dirty glass. I consulted a plastic surgeon but I think it will leave a scar regardless. We may be able to do more after it heals. The good thing is there is no real damage to your knee. You will be able to function as before."

"Oh, Dr. Wu," I said. "I don't mind a scar. A scar will help to remind me how lucky and blessed I am. And it will also remind me about the other girls who are out there somewhere and not found."

Jenny and David walked in at the moment. They looked so sweet, holding hands.

"I think we have everything over at the new house," Jenny said. "It looks very nice but you will probably want to rearrange the furniture. We put the furniture where we thought it looked nice. Also, I will unpack your dishes and kitchen stuff but you need to tell me where to put them. A lot of your dishes were broken, so we will have to go shopping and find some more."

"Oh Jenny," I said. "You have done so much; I don't know how to thank you. I can unpack myself, but it will be fun to go shopping with you."

Jenny and I walked out of the kitchen, and Jenny leaned over and whispered to me:

"I think David is going to have that talk with my Dad."

"Talk, what talk?" I replied.

"He is going to formally ask Dad for my hand in marriage," and as Jenny said this she seemed glow.

I gave her a hug with tears in my eyes. I felt so happy for my best friend. I watched as she flitted back in the kitchen. I was reminded of what a whimsical little fairy she was.

Later that evening I put Mia to sleep in her cradle and was reading when Chi came in the room.

"Chan-lei, I've been doing a lot of thinking these past few days. When I think of how close I came to losing you, my heart almost stops. You were so brave, so strong," he said.

"Chi, I wasn't brave, I was so scared, so afraid they would take Mia from me and so afraid I would never see you again. I did what anyone would do."

"You did more than anyone I know would do, you put both of those evil people in the hospital," Chi said with a laugh.

I laughed too, as I thought of Eric with a big cut and Mrs. *O'Malley* with a broken back. *They deserved it, they really did.* I said to myself. *They had threatened Mia and anyone who hurts a child deserves the worst, their own kind of hell.* I believe in forgiveness, but how could I find it in my heart to forgive them?

Chi continued to talk, "I have been thinking, you should go back to the University next semester. You are too smart not to, and now that I know how brave you are, and how much, how do you say, talent, you have, you must do something with it."

"Oh Chi," I gushed "thank you, this is what I want to do. I want to become a prosecutor like Mr. Wu, and help put bad guys in jail. But you realize it will be a lot of work. First, I have to finish college, get a degree, go to law school, pass the Bar Exam, and become an American citizen, plus take care of you and Mia."

"I know darling, but with your parents and mine here to help with Mia, I know you can do it. And I forgot to tell you, I went by the restaurant while I was out this morning to tell them I'm back and you are safe. The owner was there, and he wants to start training me for head chef. Head chef, Chan-lei, what I have always wanted.

I'm getting my dreams; why shouldn't you obtain your dreams?"

"I'm so proud of you Chi. The Sang Tung restaurant is a very upscale restaurant, not a Chinese take-out place. You will be talked about, even articles in the newspapers," I said.

"And there will be more money, I can pay for your school and you won't have to worry so much," he said pleased with himself.

After we were sure Mia was sound asleep, we went back downstairs to visit with the Wu's. I was feeling stronger now and we were so fortunate to have them as friends, not to mention, my champion and my doctor.

Mr. Wu, my champion was home and had a lot to tell me:

"Well Chan-lei, I have had a busy day. I don't know where to start. First of all, we charged Mrs. Ling today, her charges are a lot less than Eric and Mrs. O'Malley, but she will probably serve a couple of years in prison if we get a conviction. We did a search of the O'Malley house and found evidence of them holding girls there. But the best part is I found evidence to link Mrs. O'Malley to Patrick O'Malley's murder. I filed murder charges against her this afternoon and also there was a bail hearing. I recommended no bail for both of them, but the Judge set Eric's bail at $200,000.00. He held Mrs. O'Malley without bail and she will stay in jail until the trial. Eric may be able to bail out."

I didn't know what to say for a minute and then I replied. "What did you find in the house?"

"I wish I could tell you, but for now I can't until we finish with the investigation. I will tell you that the evidence we found may lead us to other girls."

"Can you find them?"

"Honestly, it will be hard to find them but we will work on it. For now, Chan-lei, I want you to be very careful. I'm having a security system put in your house, and I don't want you going out alone for a while. Remember, the men that hurt you are still out there, and Eric may be very soon," Charles said.

It wouldn't be as bad as being an actual captive, but I am still a prisoner of sorts, I thought. *but I am going back to school and my parents will be here soon. What do I have to complain about,* I thought.

Dr. Wu served a delicious dessert. She seemed to have it all, a career she loves and a wonderful family. I can do this too.

It was a lovely evening talking and then Chi and I excused ourselves and went up to bed. I was getting stronger, but I still tired easily. Mia was sleeping soundly; she must also be relieved.

About two in the morning, I woke with a start and sat straight up in bed.

"Chan-lei?" Chi said.

"I had a nightmare, it was awful," I said.

"Go back to sleep, it is not surprising you would have nightmares after what you have been through," Chi said as he snuggled closer to me.

I couldn't go back to sleep, I thought about the nightmare.

I was out with Mia, she was older, maybe four or five. We were having a good time, but suddenly it became cold and I wanted to get her home. We decided to take the city bus instead of the trolley and I felt afraid. As we stepped on the bus I felt a hand on my neck. I turned and looked into blue-eyes.

"Maybe I can't have you, but I can have her."

Will I have to look over my shoulder the rest of my life? I have two things I must do, protect my child at all costs, and find what has become of the missing girls, that I now called, *the lost girls.*

EPILOGUE

A YEAR HAS PASSED SINCE MY ABDUCTION AND RESCUE. I testified at both Eric and Mrs. O'Malley's trials. My parents arrived from China shortly after, and Chi's parents arrived a month ago. My parents found their own home, close to our house. My father took a position with an architectural firm in the city. Chi's parents are still living with us, perfect because Chi's mother looks after Mia while I attend my classes. Mia is starting to walk now and has grown so much. Chi is head chef at the Sang Tung and we are both taking classes to become citizens. Life is close to normal except for the occasional nightmares.

I sit in the courtroom between Chi and Jenny. This is the sentencing hearing for Eric. Both Eric and his mother have been found guilty of many charges, including the kidnapping of me and Mia. Mrs. O'Malley was also found guilty of conspiracy to commit murder and 1st degree murder of Patrick O'Malley. She has already been sentenced to thirty-five years to life in prison.

Two bailiffs bring Eric into the courtroom. He has both handcuffs and shackles on and is dressed in jail orange. As I look at him, I'm aware of the jagged scar on his forehead. I'm responsible for the scar! He looks disheveled, jail does not agree with him. He posted bail after the arrest but was taken back into custody after the conviction. The jury came back with the verdict in a very short time and he was declared guilty on all charges. Today he will find out his fate.

Turning around as he shuffles to his seat in the courtroom he looks straight at me with his cold blue eyes. A chill goes through me and I shudder. Chi puts his arm around me and Jenny takes my hand. I look down at the diamond on her finger, feeling better knowing life is going on despite my ordeal.

The Judge takes the bench and reads the verdict again. He then asks if anyone wishes to make a statement. I flinch but decide not to say anything. Mr. Wu gets up and delivers a talk about how horrific the crimes are and asks for the maximum penalty.

The Judge asks if the defendant wishes to make a statement. Eric's attorney stands, says yes, and gives his own statement of how Eric has always been under his mother's influence. How he never knew until he was arrested that his mother was responsible for his father's murder. He begs the judge to sentence Eric to the least amount of time.

Eric stands and begins to talk:

"I would like to say that I did these crimes of my own free will. I could have refused to go along with my mother, but I didn't. I liked the lavish lifestyle we lived. I can't blame anyone but myself. If it wasn't for Chan-lei, I would still be doing the crimes. She is the kindest and (he touched his forehead) strongest person I have ever had contact with. She did this out of love for her baby, not for herself."

Then he turns and looks at Chi, "Mr. Wah, you are the luckiest man on earth." He sits back down.

Tears roll down my cheeks, maybe the nightmares will end now.

The judge sentences Eric to fifteen years to life. He admonishes Eric to change his life and be an exemplary prisoner and he may be paroled in ten years.

We walk out of the courtroom, My ordeal is over, but it is not over for the lost girls. What can I do to save them?

ABOUT THE AUTHOR

Shirley Nolan grew up in Southern California. She is a wife, mother, and grandmother. After a career as a Court Appointed Criminal Paralegal and Investigator; handling high profile murder cases; she moved to Texas; where she worked for a major bookstore for eight years. She is now following her dream of writing full time.

www.ingramcontent.com/pod-product-compliance
Lightning Source LLC
Chambersburg PA
CBHW020056180626
46812CB00006B/2349